Long Night
Moon

SM Reine

Red Iris Books

LONG NIGHT MOON
Copyright © 2012, Red Iris Books
ISBN-13: 978-1-937733-16-2
ISBN-10: 1-937733-16-5

Red Iris Books
Website: http://redirisbooks.com/
Email: redirisbooks@gmail.com
Twitter: @redirisbooks

SM Reine
Website: http://smreine.com/
Email: smreine@gmail.com
Twitter: @smreine

Interior and cover design by Red Iris Books.

Acknowledgments

Writing is an insular practice, but I usually find ways to share the experience with friends and loved ones. Long Night Moon was the exception. Producing this book was a very lonely journey, and it almost didn't happen at all.

As such, I would be much remiss if I didn't give a nod to wiser writers than me: Krista Ball, Genevieve Clark, David Gaughran, Debora Geary, Nathan Lowell, Melissa Furrer Miller, Gordon Ryan, Phoenix Sullivan, and Michael Wallace (as well as the other refugees). You each shared advice with me when I needed it, and I may not have finished this book without your assistance. Thanks.

Books by SM Reine

*For my men,
beloved and perfect.*

Prelude

Prey

Gwyneth had run too long. She couldn't do it anymore.

Her feet slipped on the snow, and she shrieked as she tumbled down the hill. Rocks and branches battered her body. Her hands scrabbled for purchase and found nothing. She bounced over a boulder and hit the bottom in a snowdrift.

She couldn't breathe. She couldn't move.

Something approached her. The heavy thump of footfalls were like nails in the lid of a coffin, and Gwyn raised her head to stare her hunter in the face.

The wolf circled. Its hackles lifted into thick spikes, and every huffing breath fogged the frigid air. Chunks of ice stuck to its lower legs and between its paw pads, and blood matted its face.

"Please... don't do this." Gwyn's voice shook with cold and fear. A low rumble rose in the wolf's throat, lips peeling back as it stepped closer.

Gwyn hadn't believed. She had denied everything her niece said. It was impossible—full moons and werewolves and monsters. She lived in a rational world. A world of ranching. Herding, hard work. There was no such thing as magic.

But now, she believed. She believed everything.

With a growl, the wolf leaped.

Gwyn screamed. "Rylie!"

One

The Grove

Seth knew it would be a long day when he found blood in the fields.

Blood was never a good sign, since it often meant Rylie had gotten into the pastures again and eaten something she would regret. He could already hear her long speech about the innocence of cows again. It had been kind of cute... the first three times.

But this was different. He had never found so much blood after a moon. It was splattered over the frozen surface of the duck pond with a dark cherry sheen, like hard candy, and he didn't think it belonged to a cow.

The human handprints weren't a good sign, either.

He glared at his cell phone. When human bodies became involved, he had to call the police. Cops would mean an investigation, and if they saw him with a gun, he would have to answer a lot of questions.

It would be a long day. Seth hated long days.

He trudged around the duck pond in calf-deep snow, keeping the blood in his periphery. There weren't any paw prints around the pond, nor were there the other normal signs of a werewolf attack. There should have been claw marks on everything. Frenzied werewolves liked to leave marks.

Plus, there was no body. If a human died, it wasn't Rylie's fault, and that was almost worse. It meant his werewolf girlfriend wasn't the only dangerous thing in the night.

"This won't be good," he muttered.

He tracked the blood away from the pond, across the pastures, and into the fields of a neighboring farm. He picked the trail of blood up a few yards down, where it smeared for a few feet.

He didn't have to go far to find the source. Seth crossed the field and entered the thicket at its edge. Naked trees made skeleton shadows on the ground, and the fingers of the branches all pointed at one thing—the body of a farmer, half-buried in snow with his throat torn out.

Yeah. It was *definitely* going to be a long day.

Rylie would never get used to waking up outside.

She stretched out in a snowdrift, reaching her hands high over her head and flexing her toes so every muscle went taut. She felt like she had been beaten up. Her skin was battered and sore, but unmarked.

Sitting up, she peered around the fields in the light of early dawn. Snow stuck to her hair. Rylie recognized the ridge to the south, but all her normal landmarks were masked in a thick layer of snow. She had no idea whose property she was on.

And where was Seth? He usually tracked her all night so he could be close when she woke up, but there was no sign of him this time. The only footprints nearby were in the shape of wolf paws.

She got up and brushed the snow off her skin. Even though she was wet and her hair had frozen, she wasn't cold yet. The change kept her warm.

Tilting her head into the still air, she took several short sniffs. The colors of winter splashed through her mind: the chill of ice, rabbits warm in their dens, and the flowery smell of cheap perfume.

But there was another scent, too. It was the kind of smell that caught the attention of the wolf inside her, even though it should have been sleeping after a new moon.

Blood. Lots of it.

She was torn. Rylie needed her clothing before she got cold—or worse, before someone saw her streaking through the snow—but the blood smelled sticky-sweet and delicious, and she was so hungry.

Maybe just a peek.

Rylie jogged across the hills. Steam drifted off her skin and plumed around her mouth. Even though she was sleepy and sore, the call of blood made her push on.

More than a mile away, the smell became much stronger. It came from a large grove of trees.

And people were waiting on the east end.

Rylie hesitated before plunging inside. She ducked behind a thicket to keep herself hidden. Trucks with the sheriff's logo were parked nearby, as well as an ambulance, and some other vehicles with government plates.

She sniffed again. *So much blood.*

Ignoring her better instincts, Rylie crouch-walked through the grove and followed her nose.

A man in a uniform appeared on the other side of a tree.

She froze.

His back was turned, so he didn't see her. "Jesus H. Christ, what a mess," he muttered. "You ever seen something like this before, Mary?"

"What a mess," echoed a woman that Rylie couldn't see. She was blocked by a bush.

The officer moved, letting Rylie see around his legs.

At first, all she saw was meat, raw and dripping. It was laying there on the snow, waiting for someone to take it. Still fresh. Still warm. Her stomach growled so loudly that she was afraid the deputies might hear.

After a moment, her human mind kicked in.

A human body.

The man shifted again, blocking Rylie's view, but the corpse was branded into her mind. Her stomach lurched. Rylie clamped both hands over her mouth to keep from vomiting. Her shoulders heaved, and bile rose in the back of her throat. She couldn't make a noise. She couldn't get caught.

"Think it was a coyote?" Mary asked.

"Hard to say. I've never seen a coyote that vicious."

Rylie slipped out of the trees again. She felt dizzy.

Motion on the hill overlooking the grove caught her eye. A dark figure at the top waved his hand, silhouetted by the rising sun. Even though he was too far away to smell, she recognized Seth, and he disappeared as soon as she waved back.

His message was clear. Rylie had to get away from the sheriffs.

She kept low as she followed the smell of her own perfume to the clothing she had hidden between rocks a half mile away. It was far enough behind the hill that the investigators couldn't see, but she had to hurry. Finding a body meant they would probably sweep the whole area to find what killed him.

By the time she reached the rocks, her temperature started to drop, and the chill seeped into her bones. Her feet burned with cold. Her fingers became stiff and unresponsive. She hurried to pull the jeans over her legs, and they felt strange scraping over numb skin.

She had to blow on her hands until her fingers would bend before she could manage the socks and boots. Rylie skipped the shirt to put on the fur-lined jacket. She had initially refused to wear it, since she used to be a vegetarian and still hated animal products, but she was grateful for its warmth that morning.

"Sorry," she muttered through chattering teeth, trying not to imagine any poor dead bunnies.

Rylie jerked the hood over her head, stuffed the shirt into her pocket, and trudged toward the road where Seth parked the truck. They reached it at the same time.

The windows were iced over, and its hood was covered in an inch of snow. He tossed his rifle inside.

"What happened?" she asked.

He grinned when he saw her buried deep in the oversized jacket. His slanted smile made her heart stop beating for a second. Seth was wearing all black as usual, and his freshly-trimmed hair accentuated the hard lines of his cheekbones and jaw. "You're not cold, are you?"

"No," Rylie said.

"Liar."

"I'd like to see you spend all night naked one of these moons. Then we'll see who's cold."

Rylie had to move Seth's school books to get in the truck. He must have spent the night glued to his books. He was serious about semester finals, and determined to get all A's on his report card, so he didn't do much other than study.

He got in the driver's seat. She pushed back her hood.

"Seriously, Seth, what happened?"

"You saw the body. What do you think happened? Someone got killed."

"What did it?"

"I got a good look before I tipped off the sheriff. His throat had been torn out, but it was too neat to be a werewolf. They're savage when they attack," Seth said.

"You mean, *I'm* savage when I attack."

"It wasn't you. I tracked you for half the night, and you stayed out in federal lands." He didn't look at her. "And none of him had been eaten. Like I said, you're innocent."

Rylie stared at her boots. "Oh." He was right. She had gotten a few animals before, and she never left much behind. "Who died?"

"Isaiah Branson."

Her hands flew to her mouth. "My neighbor? Oh God! That's so close to my house! What if my aunt had been outside? What if—?"

Seth grabbed her hand. His touch spread warmth through her body.

"It wasn't Gwyneth, so don't worry about something that didn't happen. There's lots else to worry about anyway. If it wasn't a werewolf that tore open Branson's throat, then what was it?"

Rylie couldn't answer that. She wasn't sure she even wanted to know.

Two

Transfers

They rode back to the ranch without talking. Once the adrenaline faded, she was comfortable. A little too comfortable to stay awake, in fact. Rylie's eyes soon fell shut and she slid onto Seth's shoulder, dozing under the rumbling engine sounds.

She couldn't fall completely asleep despite her exhaustion. The memory of smells and sensations from her night as a wolf flitted through her mind. Rylie never remembered anything of the change. The more she tried to recall details, the more they slipped away. But it haunted her like a nightmare she couldn't escape.

Seth parked by Gwyn's barn and let the truck idle. "Wait here for a few minutes."

He got out. Rylie tried to relax while he did a couple chores around the ranch. Gwyn would already be awake, so she would assume an empty house meant they were out working, and she would be suspicious if they went to breakfast with nothing done.

As light crept over the fields and burned away the haze of early morning, she could make out Isaiah Branson's fence. Rylie didn't want to think of what would happen to his farm now that he was dead.

Seth fed the animals and shoveled the paths. Once he was done, he came back to the truck. "Let's go inside, Rylie. I can smell breakfast."

He half-carried her up the hill to her aunt's house. After a long night running on all fours, her muscles felt like jelly. But that wasn't really why she hung off him. She could have lived her entire life with his arm around her body. Seth was all leather and gunpowder, but he spent enough time around the ranch to pick up its familiar scents, and pressing her face into his shoulder was like smelling home.

When she caught a whiff of bacon and eggs, it perked her up in a way even Seth couldn't do. Hunger gave her enough energy to stand on her own so it wouldn't look like Seth was dragging a body into the house, which would have looked weird to Aunt Gwyneth.

But it wasn't Gwyn waiting when they entered the kitchen.

It was Seth's brother.

"Good morning, sunshines. Looks like you had a good night," Abel said.

He had made himself at home in the kitchen. He gnawed on a chunk of leftover steak while cooking bacon, sausage, and eggs on the griddle. Judging by the smell of the oven, he was making ham, too. The sight of so much meat made her mouth fill with saliva.

"What are you doing here?" Rylie asked.

"I'm cooking breakfast. What does it look like?"

It looked like one of Rylie's worst nightmares had taken over her house *again*. She couldn't get used to it. Gwyn hired him as a ranch hand after Rylie hospitalized the last one, and now Abel and Seth worked there all the time.

They were supposed to be friends now. Abel had even kind of apologized for spending half of the autumn stalking and threatening to kill her. She was still pretty sure he hated her. Rylie felt the same about him.

"Where's Gwyn?" she asked.

"Still asleep. I haven't seen her." Abel flipped an egg on the griddle and the yolk broke, oozing into a puddle of bacon grease.

Rylie took several deep breaths to settle her nerves. Finding a werewolf hunter in her kitchen right after a new moon made her adrenaline spike to ridiculous levels.

"I'm going to take a shower," she said, leaning over to kiss Seth on the cheek.

When she left the kitchen, she didn't go to the bathroom. She stood on the other side of the doorway to listen.

"What are you doing?" Seth asked.

"I said, I'm making—"

"That's not what I mean. You promised not to make trouble."

"I'm not making trouble. I'm making eggs." There was a dangerous undertone to Abel's voice.

"Were you following Rylie last night? I saw boot prints."

Abel laughed. "Listen to yourself, bro. You're paranoid. Dating a werewolf is turning you crazy."

"Oh yeah? Why else would you be here so early?"

"Gwyn asked me to come."

Whatever they said beyond that, she didn't hear it. The brothers continued their conversation in lowered voices, and she couldn't make it out over the sizzle of bacon. She dropped her boots by the woodstove and pressed her ear to her aunt's bedroom door. There was no hint of motion on the other side.

Gwyn was a total morning person. By the time the sun rose, she should have done a thousand things around the ranch and cooked a hearty breakfast.

She claimed she got sluggish during winter, but Rylie had to wonder if it wasn't something else.

Her aunt was sick. Really sick. What if it was catching up with her?

Rylie tried to purge her worries in the shower, but no amount of hot water could dislodge the sense of fear creeping over her. After she finished, she combed out her hair and dressed in leggings, boots, and a sweater that went to her knees.

When she left the bathroom, Gwyn's door was still shut.

Abel and Seth were sitting at the kitchen table when she joined them. The sight of Seth made her glow with warmth, but Abel was another story. His face was bisected by deep, cruel scars that horribly twisted his handsome profile. He had been mauled by a werewolf more than once. It was an unpleasant reminder of the damage Rylie could cause.

Seth's smile was heart-stopping. "You were in there for days. I thought you drowned."

Rylie took the chair next to him, which was as far from Abel as she could get without eating in the living room. Even though he pretended to focus on his breakfast, she could feel him watching. "Sorry. You can have a turn before we go to school. I left some hot water."

"Nah. It's fine." He pushed a plate toward her. It was heaped high with ham and sausage. "Here, I saved some from my monstrous brother."

Abel stayed silent. Rylie ate without looking at him.

When the first werewolf mauled him, Abel had been infected. There was a short period after the bite where the victim could stop the transformation, and with Seth's help, Abel hadn't become a werewolf. Some of the symptoms stuck around, though—mostly the craving for meat, an endless appetite, and serious anger issues. Between the two of them, they could have eaten an entire cow.

But Rylie wasn't as hungry as usual. "We should get to school," she said, wiping her mouth with a cloth napkin.

"Okay." Seth dropped their dishes in the sink.

"Have a good time, kids," Abel said with mock brightness. "Lots to do today! All that learning!"

Seth shoved him. "Shut up, you ugly jerk."

"Touch me again and I'll bite off your hands, dork wad."

Rylie packed leftover roast beef and boiled eggs for lunch, keeping Abel in the corner of her eye as she prepared. When he caught Rylie looking, she shot him a dirty look.

"What's taking so long?" Seth called from the front room.

She hurried to catch up.

The drive to school was long on good days. On snowy days, it was practically a road trip. It took almost an hour to do twenty miles, with nothing to look at on the way except endless sheets of white, so Rylie grabbed Seth's homework binder.

"Brainstem," she prompted.

Seth thought about it for a minute. "It keeps people alive and controls all the secondary stuff, like breathing and coughing. Right?"

She checked the back of the flash card. "Yeah. And the heartbeat, too."

"Heartbeat," he repeated. "Okay. I've got it. Give me another."

"Cerebellum."

"Is that the attention one?"

"No," Rylie said. Seth tried to peek at the back, but she pressed it to her chest. "No cheating!"

"Okay, okay." He took a deep breath and furrowed his brow. "Cerebellum. Cerebellum…" One vein stuck out on his forehead when he concentrated. Rylie thought it was cute. This was the first time Seth had tried to do an entire year of school, so she saw that vein a lot.

"It's the one that—" she began.

"Muscle memory!" he interrupted.

"You peeked."

He looked wounded. "I did not."

"You did too. I saw you."

"I wouldn't cheat. I need to know this stuff." He glared at the snowy road like it was challenging him. "I'm going to be a doctor. Maybe a brain surgeon."

"You can work on my brain whenever," Rylie said loyally.

He flashed his lopsided grin again, but it faded quickly. Seth was a senior. Even though he was taking extra classes and had good grades, he hadn't gotten any responses to his college applications. Rylie was only a junior, but she had been dutifully writing essays and applying for scholarships since she was fourteen, so she was pretty much guaranteed to go wherever she wanted.

"Studying isn't going to do much good right now anyway," Seth said. "I keep thinking about Branson."

Rylie blinked. It had only been an hour, but she completely forgot about the body. "Why? What are you thinking?"

"A wild animal didn't kill him. His hands and forearms weren't even injured. Think of it like this—what do you do if someone jumps at you?" Seth asked. Rylie bared her teeth and gave a small growl. "Okay. What do *normal* people do if something jumps at them?"

"I'm normal," she muttered sullenly.

Seth took a hand from the wheel to mimic shielding his face, arm up and palm out. "Your arm is your first line of defense. Or maybe your last. Anyway, I've seen people get attacked by dogs, and their arms get ripped up. Branson's only injury was his throat. I'm thinking he was surprised."

"Or he trusted his attacker," Rylie said.

He gave her a surprised look. "Or that."

They hit the edge of a neighborhood, and traffic made them slow down further. It never seemed like there were many people living in town until they all tried to get somewhere at the same time.

Eventually, they reached the high school. Seth parked in the empty lot at the back.

"So if it's not a werewolf, what is it?" Rylie asked.

"I don't know, but it won't stick to one kill. We'll watch for it." He rolled his eyes. "Abel's going to be psyched to have something to do."

Rylie jumped out of the truck and slammed the door behind her. The cold air nipped her cheeks, and she hurried to the warmth of his side. "Should we go to school if something's around? I mean, should you be, like... hunting?"

"Branson's killer won't be wandering around town. We'll hunt all right, but not during the day."

"What can I do to help?"

Seth took her hand and gazed at her for a long time. She noticed he was wearing a black plug in his pierced ear instead of the fang he used to have, and she wasn't sure how long it had been since she saw it. The way he looked at her made it hard to think or breathe or move at all.

He lifted the back of his hand to her lips. "You're amazing," he whispered. Seth's breath was warm on her skin, and her cheeks flamed with heat.

"Shut up," she mumbled. "You know how much that embarrasses me."

He laughed and pulled her against his body. Even with a half dozen layers of clothing between them, a thrill of excitement raced through her. She wasn't used to having a boyfriend, much less someone like Seth. They were usually too busy to have fun, but when they did, it was better than she could have imagined.

He bent down to kiss her, and Rylie stretched up on her toes. Someone cleared their throat behind her.

Her thoughts went murderous and black. She couldn't help but growl. "What?" she snapped, shooting a nasty look over her shoulder.

The dean of students waited by the fence in a bulky jacket and earmuffs. "I don't think I need to remind you two about our policy on public displays of affection. *Again*."

"Good thing we aren't at school yet," Seth said. Rylie felt like she had to straighten her clothes even though they hadn't done anything.

"This is your third warning this week. Next time, it's detention—separately. Get to class."

Sometimes, Rylie wished she had eaten Dean Block on All Hallows' Eve.

She got her knapsack out of the truck and stalked through the fence. The dean watched them go inside before shutting the gate behind them.

They trudged to the quad. The lonely tree was naked of leaves, and icicles hung off its highest branches. "I'll see you at lunch," Seth said. Dean Block was still watching them, so he squeezed her hand to say goodbye.

She was the last person to arrive in her English class, and all the students were whispering around a desk in the front. This was nothing new. Ever since Rylie and Seth started publicly dating, people whispered about them constantly. They were basically school celebrities.

But this time, nobody looked at her when she came in. The teacher didn't even acknowledge Rylie as she took her seat. She shoved her knapsack under the chair and realized she still had the flashcards.

"Hypothalamus," Rylie murmured, reading the one on top before flipping it over. Seth's sharp, slanted handwriting said "body temperature, appetite, hormone signaling." She bet that if her boyfriend did operate on her brain, he would find the werewolf crouched where the hypothalamus should be.

Maybe Rylie should have been the one skipping school to hunt for bad guys. The wolf gave her an amazing sense of smell, even as a human. She could probably track by scent.

But Seth was right. The killer wouldn't just be wandering around.

The bell rang, and the teacher stood.

"Take your seats. We have a couple announcements this morning. First of all, the leadership committee wants everyone to know that the date of the Winter Ball has been changed from the sixteenth to the twenty-third. You can still buy tickets at the front office."

Rylie's stomach pitched. She'd been trying not to think about the dance since it was announced, but it was hard, considering that glitter-drenched blue posters had been plastered everywhere. The smaller rural schools were throwing it together. Hundreds of kids would be there—more people than there were at Rylie's whole school, in fact.

Seth hadn't asked her to go yet, but the change in date was bad. The new moon was the night of the twenty-third.

"Secondly, as you've already discovered, we have a new student today. Bekah, could you please stand?"

A girl rose from her desk at the front of the classroom.

Bekah turned to face everyone. She had a hooked nose, cascades of golden-brown curls, and a big smile with white teeth. A pendant shaped like a five pointed star dangled from a chain around her neck.

Shock jolted through Rylie. Bekah's eyes were bright gold.

"Hi everyone. I'm Rebecca Riese. I just moved here from California, and I can't wait to get to know you."

She stared at Rylie in the back of the class while she spoke, as though there was nobody else in the room. Rylie knew with total certainty that Seth wouldn't have to hunt for Isaiah Branson's killer after all.

Bekah was a werewolf.

Three

Honey

Rylie's fingertips itched. She looked down to see spots of blood oozing at the edges of her nails. Underneath, the hard points of knife-sharp claws were emerging.

She gasped and stuffed her hands into her lap.

Bekah's mouth moved. She was still talking, using human lips to make human sounds, but Rylie couldn't understand any of it. White noise filled her skull.

Now that she had seen Bekah's eyes, her smell was overwhelming—snow, soil, pine, icy rivers, cold stone. Rylie knew that odor because it was hers, too. It was the smell of Gray Mountain, the place where she had been turned into a werewolf.

The wolf rose in her gut at the smell of a challenger. Rylie's body seized, and she bowed her head against the strength of it.

She shouldn't have been able to change. Not during the day. *Not here.*

The teacher sorted papers at her lectern. The students were entranced by the allure of a new student. Nobody saw Rylie's internal battle except Bekah, and her expression didn't change. She wasn't surprised to see Rylie in so much pain.

"I can't wait to get to know everyone," Bekah finished with a throaty giggle. Demon. Wolf. Murderer.

Rylie shoved her chair back so hard the desk fell over. The distance between class and the bathroom was a blur. She slammed the handicapped stall door shut, threw the latch, and slid down the wall to sit on cold tile.

What were the odds that one of those things would show up the morning after a farmer's murder and have nothing to do with it? Rylie sucked at math, but she bet the odds were somewhere between "ridiculous" and "basically impossible."

She clenched her hands in her hair and pressed her face against her knees.

Another female. A challenger. Competition for territory.

Rylie's mind flooded with images of tearing out Bekah's throat, just like the farmer's had been. She could make it fast. It wouldn't even be a fight. Then she would leave Bekah somewhere to tell other wolves that this was *her* home, and they needed to stay away.

"Stop it," she hissed, but the harder she tried not to think about hurting Bekah, the clearer her visions became.

She *had* to do it. She couldn't be driven off her land.

The claws curved over her fingertips now. She wouldn't even have to change all the way to kill.

She clenched her fists. Her hands throbbed as the claws dug into her palms. *What am I thinking?*

"Seth," she whispered into the empty bathroom, like saying his name would make him appear. It helped to imagine him watching. What would he think if she changed into a werewolf in the girl's bathroom? What would he say about her murderous thoughts?

Rylie stuffed her hands into her pockets and hurried outside the building. The clouds blocked out the sun and turned everything gray.

She found Seth's classroom and peeked her head in the window, scanning the desks until she saw him in the far corner.

The class was darkened for a movie, and she could see the teacher talking on his cell phone in the hallway beyond.

Seth didn't notice her waving through the glass. Rapping a claw on the window made several heads turn, but not his. A girl behind him recognized Rylie and kicked his chair.

He shot a glance at the teacher before hurrying to the door. She grabbed his arm and dragged him toward the truck.

"Whoa, slow down a minute. What's wrong?" Seth asked.

"I found it," she whispered.

"What? What did you find?"

"The killer." She barely moved her lips when she spoke. Rylie's hearing was incredible, so Bekah's would be, too. She didn't want the other werewolf to pick up what she was saying.

He looked down and saw her hand smearing blood on his coat. His eyes widened.

"Jesus, Rylie!" Seth dragged her behind a bush where they couldn't be seen.

"It's another werewolf. I got so angry, I couldn't stop myself—and oh my God, I started *changing*. I managed to wait until I was alone, but—"

He grabbed her wrists. "Okay, stop. Take a deep breath. You have to calm down."

"How am I supposed to calm down? There's another werewolf, Seth!"

"Shh," he said. "Not so loud."

She dropped her voice to a whisper. "That must have been who killed the farmer. That's why it happened so close to my house. I'm going to kill her. I have to do it."

"Rylie!" Seth shook her by the shoulders, and she cut off. "Listen to me. You don't want to kill anyone. That's the wolf talking. We've been over this before—you have to stay in charge or it's going to rule you. Don't let it." Rylie nodded, eyes blurred with tears. "Deep breath."

It took three tries, but she managed to fill her lungs and let it out slowly. Seth watched her closely until she felt her face relax and her shoulders slump.

Her fingertips burned. When she looked down, the claws were gone. "Oh my God," she whispered. "I could have changed in class and killed everyone." There were no words to comfort her, so he hugged her, and she squeezed back, careful not to hold too tightly. "How did you get so good at this?"

Seth gave a shrug like it was no big deal, but she could tell the answer bothered him. He dropped his gaze. "Abel talked like that when he was changing. He was hung up on killing everyone who pissed him off." He switched subjects. "Okay, who is it?"

"It's the new student. We met this morning."

"You mean Levi Riese?"

"Who's Levi?" Rylie asked.

"The new student. I guess Coach invited him to join the football team."

Rylie didn't like the sound of that at all. "When you and your family were hunting werewolves, how did you find them? Did they hang out on their own like me, or do they come in packs?"

"Families," Seth said, releasing her hands. "It's usually families, not packs. Like two or three of them at a time. A dad and son, cousins... or siblings."

"The werewolf I saw isn't Levi. Her name is Bekah—Bekah Riese. She has eyes like mine." Rylie gnawed on her bottom lip. "I bet they're *both* werewolves. What are we going to do?"

A voice spoke from behind them. "You're going back to class."

Rylie braced herself before turning, expecting Dean Block to be waiting with a detention slip.

She wasn't prepared to see Bekah Riese with all her honey curls and a sparkling smile.

Her hackles lifted. Seth stepped in front of her.

"What do you want?" he asked.

"That's a pretty deep question for someone I just met. What do I want? What does everyone want? I bet it's the same thing." Bekah faltered under his hard stare. Her smile faded. "Seriously, you both need to get back to class. I told the teacher Rylie is sick, but she'll come looking if we don't get back soon."

"Why would you lie for her? You don't even know anything about us," Seth said.

"I know a lot more than you think."

The wind shifted, wafting Bekah's smell toward her. Rylie tried to move forward, but Seth blocked her with his body. He shifted so that she couldn't even see Bekah.

He lowered his voice. "Did you kill him?"

Rylie would have given anything to see Bekah's face in that moment. When the other girl spoke, she sounded genuinely confused by the question. "What are you talking about?"

She was pretending. She had to be.

"You know what I mean," he said.

"I'm going back now. You guys should, too," Bekah said.

Her footsteps moved away from them, crunching in the snow. Rylie sagged against Seth's back, wrapping her arms around his stomach, but he didn't face her until Bekah was gone. "She's right," he said.

"Are you serious? You expect me to go to class and ignore the werewolf in the front row?"

"No." Seth glanced over his shoulder, like he was checking for Bekah. His hearing wasn't as good as Rylie's. She had already heard the door to the building open and shut again. "But you can't ditch. The dean's already out to get us. Can you do that? Can you get through class?"

Rylie bit her lip, but nodded. "If I have to."

"Get through today. That's all." He gripped her hand hard. "You can do it."

It was nice one of them was so confident.

Four

Maidenhair

Bekah wasn't in any of Rylie's other classes, but she still spent the afternoon glancing over her shoulder and around corners like she expected the other werewolf to jump out.

"Dude, what's wrong with you?" Tate asked.

Rylie was slouched over her desk and bouncing her knee at a rate of about a million times a second. The teacher hadn't bothered telling her to put down her hood.

Tate's family was rich and important, so people didn't call him out on his misbehaviors, and his friendship gave Rylie some immunity. But Tate was a special kind of untouchable. In fact, he had been arrested twice since Halloween and still hadn't seen a judge.

"What are you talking about?" she asked.

"You look freaked out. What did you take?"

Rylie made herself stop joggling her leg. "Nothing."

"Then that's your problem for sure," he said wisely. She laughed. It was the first time she had laughed all day, and it made the knot in her chest loosen a little. "Are you coming over tomorrow? I've got the new Dark Crash Exodus game. The guys and me are going to stay up until we beat it."

"You're doing multiplayer? In person?"

"We can't share snacks over the internet." Which was Tate's way of saying "we're going to try out my new gravity bong." Rylie pulled a face. Her nose was too sensitive for that.

"I have stuff to do at the ranch. Sorry."

But Rylie didn't go home at the end of the day. She had appointments with a therapist Fridays after school—no exceptions. The visits became required after she tried to tell her aunt she was a werewolf. She skipped out on the first couple of sessions, but Gwyn put a stop to that by threatening to kick her out of the house, and her attendance had been perfect since.

She normally walked to therapy, but the snow was deep, so Seth dropped her off. Riding with him wasn't as nice as usual. He was too distracted to even kiss her goodbye.

Janice Brown was a frail woman with gray hair to her waist, a love of gardening, and an obsession with chess. She had the board ready when Rylie showed up. "Do you want to be white or black this time?"

"Black," Rylie said. She always asked to be black. The pieces were prettier.

"How was school?"

"Fine."

Rylie sat on a worn yellow stool. Once Janice finished watering her ferns, she took the other seat. "This time of year is hard on the plants. The air is so dry." She moved her pawn, and Rylie moved her knight. "It would help my plants to get more attention throughout the week."

"Have your secretary do it."

After a moment of contemplation, Janice moved another pawn. She was obviously clearing space for her rook to get into play. "Christina has enough to worry about. Two other therapists use this office during the week, and it's a scheduling nightmare."

"So ask one of the other therapists," she said.

Janice gave a little smile. "Maybe someone will volunteer."

"I'm going to take your pawn if you don't move it."

"Even though it will endanger your knight?"

She took the pawn. Janice took her knight. It gave Rylie the chance to kill another pawn, though, so it wasn't all bad. She didn't care anyway. It was hard to get upset about a stupid board game when there were werewolves on the loose.

"Your bishop is next," Rylie warned.

"I don't think so."

Janice took her queen. She stared at the board. She hadn't even seen it was in danger.

They played on without talking for a few minutes, but that only made the misery of losing to Janice worse. Of course, after about ten weeks of therapy and not a single win, it wasn't a surprise.

Checkmate. New game.

This time, Rylie played white. She started out moving all her pawns like a wall, but that strategy didn't faze the therapist any more than her aggressive knight maneuvers.

"Tell me about school this week. Have you and Seth made plans for the Winter Ball?" Janice asked.

The very mention of it was enough to make her cheeks hot. "He would ask me if he wants to go."

"Do you think dancing embarrasses him?"

Rylie stared at the board without really seeing it. They had sort of gone to a dance together at summer camp, and he hadn't seemed embarrassed then. "I don't think that's the problem."

The therapist's pieces were sweeping the board. She managed to protect her king with a rook and bishop, but her numbers dwindled.

"He's on the football team, isn't he?"

"Yeah, and half the other guys in school. Everyone's going. I don't think he's trying to hide from them or anything."

"Then what?" Janice asked.

It's on the same night I'll turn into a werewolf.

She didn't say that out loud. Rylie didn't need to be taken to a mental hospital again. "There are new kids at school," she said, just to change the subject.

"How exciting." One of Janice's pawns was about to become a queen. "I grew up in a town this size. We only saw new people every few years, and it was always an event. What do you think of them?"

Murderers. Challengers. Enemies.

"I don't know."

Janice's queen moved. Check. Rylie's king could only go in one direction, so she sent her remaining knight to save him, but it was too late.

Checkmate.

Rylie slouched back. "This game sucks. It's not fair. You should let me win sometimes."

"Why? I don't like to lose anymore than you do." Janice started dropping the pieces back in their box. "This is the last time we'll get to play for a couple of weeks, so you can beat me when I get back. I'm visiting my family for Christmas. Do you have anything planned?"

Rylie grimaced. Her mom, Jessica, had demanded a visit over winter break. Considering the new moon was right before Christmas, she refused. Instead, Jessica planned on coming down for New Years, and she wanted to meet Seth.

"I'm staying home," she mumbled.

Janice closed the box and latched it. "One of my colleagues from California is visiting the practice while I'm gone. He'll fill in for me. What do you think of that?"

"I think I shouldn't have to go to therapy during the holidays," Rylie said.

"Just one more visit. Next week."

Rylie opened her mouth to say no, but then she remembered Gwyn's threat. "One more week, and then nothing else until January?" Janice nodded. "Fine. Whatever."

"My ferns are going to need help for the month I'm gone. Will you water them once a week? We're only a quarter mile from your school, and Christina can take care of them the rest of the time."

"Not a chance."

Janice smiled. "I'll pay you for babysitting."

"You just want me to keep checking in while you're gone." The older woman shrugged. Rylie rolled her eyes. "Okay, I guess."

"Wonderful. I'll leave care instructions next to the maidenhair." She gave Rylie a quick hug, so fast that she couldn't fight back. Janice smelled like sage and jasmine. "Can I give you a piece of advice?"

"That's your job, isn't it?"

"Don't wait for Seth to invite you to the Winter Ball. You're a modern woman. Take the initiative." Janice gave a smile and a wink, then ushered Rylie out of the office to take the next teenage delinquent.

Outside, the world was hushed by snow. A plow crept past flashing yellow lights. Rylie stuffed her hands into her pockets, scanning for Seth and the truck.

He wasn't there, but someone else waited across the street in a long white jacket. Bekah.

"What do you want?" Rylie asked without raising her voice. A werewolf's hearing wasn't as good as its smell, but it was better than a human's. She would have been able to hear a whisper at that distance.

"I want to talk to you," she said, toying with the star necklace so it caught the light and flashed at Rylie. "Come with me. We've got lots to cover and not a lot of time."

She shook her head. "I don't want anything to do with you. Get out of my town!"

"Please? It's important."

"No!"

Bekah tucked the necklace into her jacket. "Look me up when you change your mind. But don't take long. You're not safe here."

She walked away, jacket trailing behind her.

A burst of curiosity struck Rylie. She wanted to see Bekah Riese's den. No, not den—people didn't live in dens; they lived in *houses*. But as soon as the thought crossed her mind, it became an uncontrollable impulse.

Rylie ran across the street. She hit a patch of hidden ice and slipped, catching herself on the lamp post.

The other girl vanished around the corner of a bakery. By the time she found her footing and made it to the sidewalk, Bekah was gone. A huge, shaggy dog with honey-brown fur trotted away, fluffy tail leaving swishing patterns in the snow.

It glanced at her from the end of the street. Even at that distance, Rylie could see its gold eyes.

It bounded over a fence, down a hill, and disappeared.

Rylie gaped at the gray sky. The sun was up and the moon was nowhere to be seen.

How could a werewolf transform during the day?

Five

Casting Silver

When Seth still hadn't shown up twenty minutes after Bekah's weird disappearance, Rylie decided to find him.

Like everything else in town, the apartment Abel rented was a short walk from the therapist's office. The complex had been converted from a strip motel, so there were only six rooms, and the sign said there were vacancies (though the neon had died years ago). The red truck was parked in front of the apartment at the end, and it was already coated in a thin layer of snow.

Rylie raised her fist to knock on the door before she noticed it was cracked open. Warm air gusted through the gap at the bottom. A foul odor touched her nose, metallic and familiar.

"Seth?" she called, pushing the door open.

The owners left the tacky carpet when they converted it, so the room still looked like a motel despite the sixty-inch TV Abel bought with his first paycheck. The bathroom door was half-open, too, and the smell grew worse as she approached it.

Something hissed beyond the door. She covered her mouth with her hand, trying not to throw up.

There was a camp stove in the bathtub. Leaping blue flames licked the bottom of a steel pot, where the horrible smell was coming from. Another pot sat next to the tub filled with bars of gray metal, like the kind of ingots she expected to find at a bank.

A bunch of tools were laid out on the counter—thick gloves, eye goggles, a face mask, and tongs. There was also something that looked like the molds she once used to make candy, but she doubted it was for chocolate.

She heard the apartment door open and shut.

"Get out of there!"

Seth slammed into the bathroom. Shocked, she took a step back. Her leg hit the pot and she lost balance.

He grabbed her arm before she could fall into the tub, fingers digging into her skin. "Let go of me," Rylie said as he jerked her back. "That hurts!"

Seth hauled her out of the bathroom and shut the door, wheeling around to grab her shoulders and look closely at her face. "What are you doing? Are you *insane*?"

"You didn't show up when my appointment finished. I got worried."

"Look at me, Rylie. Eyes wide open," he said.

The order was so confusing that all she could do was obey. He thumbed back her eyelids and peered into her eyes. He looked worried. Really worried. "What was all that stuff?" she asked.

"You can't buy silver bullets at the store," Seth said.

He pushed her to the kitchen sink and scrubbed her hands under hot water.

"You mean you were making bullets?"

"Yeah, and what if you inhaled silver particles? You shouldn't have gone in there." He released her, and Rylie's knees were so weak that she had to sit on the edge of his futon before she fell over. "I think you're fine. We got lucky."

Rylie had been shot with a silver bullet before. It was the most painful thing she ever experienced. Werewolves couldn't heal around silver, and if it stayed in the bloodstream, it was poisonous. She didn't want to think of what would happen if she breathed it into her lungs.

She wiped her hands on her jeans just in case. "Why would you make something that can kill me?"

"It's not for you," Seth said. He looked uncomfortable.

She bit her lip and ducked her head. Knowing he made silver bullets shouldn't have surprised her—the whole reason they met was because he hunted the werewolf who bit her, after all—but it did. It was an unpleasant shock.

He knelt in front of her. "You have to be careful in my apartment. Abel and I have a lot of things that can kill you." Seth frowned. "Are you crying?"

Rylie swiped at her eyes with the back of her hand. "I saw Bekah again. She was waiting for me when I got out of my appointment."

"What did she want?"

"I don't know. She was just… waiting. And that's where it got weirder." She picked at her thumbnail, trying to decide if she should tell him what she saw, even though it was impossible.

"How weird?"

She shook her head. "It sounds nuts."

"All of this is nuts."

Good point. "Bekah transformed. She turned a corner and… poof. Wolf. It took five seconds." Rylie gave him a helpless smile. "It's not possible. I must have lost it."

Seth's expression went distant with thought. She waited for him to say something insightful—to explain how it was possible for someone to become a wolf without all the screaming and pain involved in her transformation, or how she had to be mistaken. But he only looked thoughtful.

"So? What are we going to do about it?" she asked.

He shook himself. "You need to go home. Gwyn's waiting for you."

"But—"

"I have to finish the bullets while everything is hot. You can't be here."

He walked her to the truck. Rylie got in, but didn't immediately close the door. "Will you tell me before you hunt them?"

Seth grinned his lopsided grin. "Maybe."

He shut her door and went inside without waiting for her to leave. Rylie's hands squeezed tight on the steering wheel.

She was halfway home before she realized what was so wrong about Bekah and the star on her necklace.

It was silver.

• ◗ •

Abel's car was parked out front when she got home, but he was nowhere to be seen. Gwyneth sat on the living room floor surrounded by boxes labeled "Christmas Decorations" in permanent marker, although none of them were open yet.

"You're late," her aunt said without preamble. Her eyes were rimmed with dark circles, and she had knotted her graying hair into a simple bun instead of the usual braids.

"I had my appointment today."

"That ended over an hour ago."

"The weather was bad coming back, so I drove slow," Rylie said. "Aren't you always telling me to be careful?"

"Guess I am. Grab something sharp and help me open these things."

She fetched two knives from the kitchen and handed one to Gwyn. The boxes exploded musty air when sliced open. Ryle breathed in the distant holiday odors of years past: pine and gingerbread and nutmeg.

"That smells nice," she said.

"What does?"

Rylie took a second sniff. It was probably too faint for Gwyn to pick up. She forgot most people didn't smell like she did. "Never mind. These boxes are really dusty."

"I didn't decorate last year. Or the year before. I've never been much for Christmas, but it doesn't seem right to let it pass unobserved now you're here." Gwyn smiled wryly. "And I know Jessica's going to expect a big Christmas when she arrives."

Rylie rolled her eyes. The less she thought about her mom's impending visit, the better. "I'm going to Australia for the rest of the year. I've just decided."

"Only if I can go with you." She liked Jessica even less than Rylie did.

"It's a deal."

They emptied the box of knotted Christmas lights first. Gwyn untangled them on the couch while Rylie hung garland. She tried not to notice how gaunt her aunt looked. She had lost a lot of weight recently and was completely lost in her sweater.

Rylie glanced through the window as she decorated, half-expecting Bekah to be lurking outside. The only person she saw in the fields was Abel, but he wasn't much better.

"What's Abel been doing here all day?" Rylie asked. "He was in the kitchen at breakfast this morning."

"I asked him to come."

"Why?"

"Because he's my employee and I can do that," Gwyn said. "Two particularly ambitious heifers birthed today. He helped."

"But you always do that stuff yourself. Why are you inside if we're calving, anyway? You can't tell me the snow bothers you."

Gwyn shoved the first strand of lights into her arms. "Put that over the window."

Her tone of voice left no room for questions. It meant Gwyn considered the topic to be none of her business, and pushing it would probably get her "volunteered" for an awful chore. Considering half their cows were pregnant, Rylie could see herself shoulder-deep in birthing fluids way too easily. She didn't want to find out how much a cow would panic over a werewolf midwife.

"Should Seth help too?" Rylie asked.

"I've got his number if I need him. That boy has a lot of homework that needs to come first." Gwyn cast a sideways look at her. "Speaking of homework..."

She sighed. "But it's *Friday.*"

"I wouldn't put off my work if I was you. Did you know the dean of students called me this afternoon? Your grades are slipping."

"Isn't that supposed to be confidential?"

"Your flesh is mine until you're eighteen, babe." Gwyn gave an evil chuckle, and Rylie tried not to make a face.

The front door opened with a blast of cold air. Abel's towering form filled the doorway as snow gusted around his feet. His scarred face was covered by a scarf. "Rylie," he began, and then he noticed Gwyneth. His tone changed. "Afternoon. What's going on here?"

"We're decorating. What are your thoughts on scaling very tall ladders to hang lights?" Gwyn asked.

"Depends on how much you're paying me. Can I talk to you outside, Rylie?" He kept his tone casual, but she detected a hint of urgency.

She dropped the Santa Claus potholders on the coffee table. "Sure," she said, trying to sound equally casual, even though being asked to talk by Abel sent her into panic mode. Had something happened? Was Seth hurt?

"Don't be long," Gwyn said. "Dinner's soon."

"I'm just going to show her something. Won't be long at all," Abel said.

Rylie pulled on a hat and gloves and followed him outside. It took her three steps to match each of his long-legged strides, and he didn't wait for her to keep up.

His smells enveloped her even though she stayed well out of arm's reach. In some ways, he resembled Seth. They shared that gunpowder smell, and the faint tang of stomach-churning silver. But even though he had never been to Gray Mountain, he had that smell of cold stone and ice rivers, too.

She was so distracted by Abel's odor that she didn't notice where they were going. He stopped at the duck pond and looked at her expectantly. The scarred side of his face was pale with cold.

"What?" she asked.

He waved in the general direction of the pond. "There. Can't you tell?"

Rylie looked again. Abel's boot prints flattened the snow, and tire tracks crossed the field from the gate toward the trees. She stepped closer to gaze at the ice. The wind shifted.

And that was when the smell struck her.

"Bekah," she said.

"Who?"

"Bekah Riese." She took several short sniffs. Pictures splashed through her mind—thick fur, pine trees, and silver. There were two distinct creatures, and she didn't know the second. "I think her brother was here, too."

Rylie tracked the smells around the pond. They were a few hours old. Bekah and Levi must have explored during the night, while the moon was high. She followed their traces to the top of a nearby hill.

When she turned around, she could see the house perfectly. Had they watched her transform?

Abel was right behind her. "You say Bekah and Levi Riese are the new werewolves. Are you *sure* that's them?" She hesitated before nodding. "I'm serious. How sure are you?"

She swallowed hard. "Deadly sure."

"They're on our territory," Abel said.

Something about the way he growled *territory* struck a chord within her. She could feel the wolf press against the inside of her ribs.

"They need to die," she whispered.

Abel grinned.

They didn't talk as they walked back to the house. He stopped her from going inside with a hand on the door.

"We can't do it yet. We've got to wait for the moon. Understand what I'm saying?"

"I understand."

That was their family's rule. They only hunted on the full and new moon and wouldn't shoot anything that wasn't four-legged and furry. It was supposed to prevent mistakes.

They stood outside for a few seconds too long. Time stretched awkwardly between them. She dropped her gaze first, staring at the toes of her boots.

"Seth's making bullets," she added.

He nodded. "Good."

She went inside. Abel followed.

Rylie smiled like they had been talking about something funny, but murder wasn't funny.

"Hey, I think I'm going to go..." Rylie began before trailing off. Gwyn's back was turned. She gripped the phone against her ear. "What's wrong?"

Her face was drawn into a grimace when she turned around. "That was Joseph calling. The farmer two miles down. He wanted us to know Isaiah Branson is dead." Gwyn set the receiver down.

Rylie tried to look surprised. "Oh my God," she said, and it sounded flat. She cleared her throat and tried again. "What happened?"

"Animal attack." Gwyn braced herself against the table, brow furrowing with pain. "We should... I need to..." She pressed a hand against her forehead. Her lips were colorless.

Rylie reached for her. "Gwyn—"

She held up a hand, keeping her niece back. "I have pies in the freezer, and butternut squash soup. We'll drop off some food. Shouldn't have to cook when you're in mourning."

"I'll drive," Abel said.

She expected Gwyn to argue. After years of running her own little ranch, she was more likely to pull a shotgun on someone trying to baby her than agree to it.

But this time, she nodded.

"All right. Rylie, grab some food. I'll meet you two at the truck in five minutes."

Six

Mourning

They listened to the radio as they drove to the Branson farm. At first, the station played slow, boring Christmas music, which was like dripping acid into Rylie's ears, but it was even worse when the local news took over.

"Efforts by rangers to curb the coyote population have doubled in response to animal attacks. Volunteer hunters will be on patrol to thin their numbers. If you would like to volunteer for—"

Rylie punched the power button.

"I ought to volunteer," Gwyn said thoughtfully. "Get back at those coyotes for eating my chickens."

"They were dumb birds anyway," Rylie muttered. It hadn't been a coyote that got into her coop.

Isaiah's wife didn't answer the door when they rang the bell. Gwyn and Rylie waited on the stoop, arms filled with frozen pies and bags of soup.

She had never been to the neighbor's farm as a human before. It was surreal. The Branson house looked a lot like theirs—a squat brown thing with a chicken coop on the side and a horseshoe over the door. But they had no Christmas lights. Everything was dark with mourning.

Rylie glanced back at the truck, where Abel leaned against the tailgate. She didn't want to be there. "Maybe they aren't home."

A moment later, the door opened. The kid who answered had red eyes and a blank expression. "Yeah?"

"Hello, Elijah," Gwyn said. "Is your mama here?"

The shift in air brought powerful smells to Rylie's nose. Cleaning fluid. Strange people. The salt of tears. Her sensitive ears perked up at the sounds of crying, and it made her hungry. All that weak, unsuspecting prey...

No, not prey. Just a grieving family.

Her human and wolf sides grappled with each other. It made her dizzy. "I'm not feeling good," she whispered.

Gwyn nodded and shifted the rest of the pies into her arms. Elijah Branson let her inside, and Rylie backed off the doorstep, offering him a tight smile that he didn't return. Of course not. His dad was dead.

She sat on the fence separating their garden from the fields. A bushy-tailed black cat darted past with its ears flattened to its skull. The wolf didn't want to give chase this time. Rylie buried her face in her hands.

Her dad was dead, too. He had a heart attack while she was at summer camp, horrible and sudden and completely natural. The doctor used to say he ate too many fatty foods. They talked about eventual heart surgery once or twice, but nobody thought it was urgent. They didn't expect it to be fatal so soon.

Becoming a werewolf and working on Gwyn's ranch was the best distraction she could have hoped for. If she was looking forward to the next moon, she couldn't think about how her dad wouldn't be at graduation, help her pick a college, or walk down the aisle when she got married.

But Isaiah Branson's kids were a lot younger than Rylie. What were they supposed to do without their father?

She scrubbed her hand over her eyes, trying to make herself stop crying so she could go inside. But it wouldn't stop. Once she started thinking about her dad, it was like falling into a deep black pit with no surface.

Abel pushed off the truck and headed toward her.

The thought of having to talk to him was too much. Rylie jumped over the fence and headed toward the fields, taking deep breaths to steady herself. Every time she sucked in a breath, it caught in her throat and made her shoulders jerk.

"Hey!"

Not now, Rylie thought, silently cursing Abel with the kind of words that would have made Gwyn smack her.

He came up and clapped a hand on her shoulder. She managed to squeeze out one word between sobs: "*What?*"

Abel gave an impatient huff. "Stop crying."

Even Rylie's responding growl was weak. "Shut up," she said instead.

"Yeah. I'm terrified."

Her face heated and her chin trembled. She turned around so she wouldn't have to see him.

Rylie thought he might go away if she ignored him, but he didn't take the hint. He waited. After a few minutes of awkwardly staring at the corn until her eyes dried, she faced him.

"What do you want?"

"You should know Branson's not the only one who died," Abel said. His eyes glowed with anticipation. "Some guy named Gates was killed, too. The neighbors are talking about it."

She wiped her runny nose on her sleeve. She wouldn't have done it in front of Seth, but she didn't care if Abel thought she was gross. "Gates. I don't know that name."

"He's a librarian who lives in Turner's Crossing fifty miles north of here. The cops said he took his dog out to use the bathroom and got attacked. Both of them dragged off and killed."

"Fifty miles? That's too far for the same killer."

"So you think there's two things ripping out throats and leaving the bodies intact? Really? Are you that stupid?"

She thought of Bekah and Levi. Even though she hadn't seen the brother yet, she was starting to form a mental image involving lots of body hair, glistening fangs, and dripping blood. "There could be two, but I would have thought they hunted together."

"Maybe they're really fast. We'll have fun with that."

"I don't think Seth wants me to hunt them," she said.

"He's naïve. Territory disputes between werewolves get bad fast. You'll hunt them all right, no matter what my white knight of a brother thinks. All I've got to do is follow you and pull the trigger."

Rylie shivered. "Who's the gun going to be pointing at when you start shooting?"

Abel started back toward the truck. When he passed her, he leaned down to whisper in her ear.

"The big bad wolf."

Abel's classic Chevy Chevelle was like their family history on four wheels. He had bought it for his sixteenth birthday using money he scraped together doing odd jobs, and it immediately became home away from home.

The upholstery on the back of the passenger's seat had patches to cover claw marks from the werewolf they killed in Grand Rapids. The trunk was dented from the time they abducted a woman mid-transformation and took her into the woods to finish her off. There were cigarette burns from Seth's brief rebellious smoking phase (which ended when Abel smacked him so hard that his eyeballs almost flew from his skull), and there was even a gun safe installed underneath the back seats.

But now they had an actual home, and the car was getting a break. "Home" might have been three hundred fifty square feet in an old motel, but it was theirs—and it was starting to develop its own history.

Molten silver was stuck to the grout between tiles. There was gun grease on the faucets. Seth's corner was stacked with text books, school papers, binders, and anatomy posters. Even that horrible perfume Rylie used lingered on their cheap furniture.

All those things added up. When Seth came in the front door after a visit to the library, it made something inside of him unwind. Nothing else made him relax like that except the Chevelle.

After Seth loaded magazines with his newly-cast and greased silver bullets, he tossed them into a black bag he kept under his futon and shoved everything out of the way. He wouldn't be able to focus on studying until the apartment was clean, and he needed to ace his anatomy finals.

But where to start? Seth stared at the binders and folders strewn across his floor and felt a sense of helplessness. He'd never worked on a deadline. He hadn't been graded before, either.

So he pushed those aside and focused on what he *did* know how to do.

"Maps," he muttered, unloading his backpack. He had visited the library while Rylie was in therapy. "Books. Articles... crime reports... school records." Four neat stacks on his bed.

He hung the map on the wall over his futon. It had been copied out of a local history book, which depicted the local area in minute detail. It hadn't been easy to find. Most maps didn't even dignify their little town with a dot on a road.

Seth jammed a single pin into the wall.

Levi and Bekah Riese's house. There was no better place to get started.

Doubt filled him as he stared at the pin. He reached into his pocket to wrap his fist around the werewolf fang he used to wear as an earring and pressed his thumb against the razor-sharp tip until it stung. He was careful not to break the skin.

Seth didn't want to find out if a dead werewolf could transfer the curse.

The hunt that earned him that fang was unforgettable. He tracked the werewolf for six months. It was a homeless guy who moved around a lot. Crazy. Deranged.

When Seth finally planted a bullet in his furry skull, he had never been so satisfied. And killing something—someone—who murdered so many people *should* have been satisfying… shouldn't it?

But now Seth imagined every werewolf looking like Rylie, and he wondered what would have happened to her if he hadn't been there to help when she first changed. Would she have gone crazy, too?

Everything had been so much easier when he knew werewolves were the bad guy.

He abandoned his research on the bed. His mother, Eleanor, would have been disappointed. Once she started the process of tracking down her "prey," she didn't stop until she finished. But Seth never could have lived up to her expectations.

Seth found himself leaving the apartment and walking toward the Riese house anyway. It wasn't far. They had bought a little brick house on the edge of town with a white picket fence.

He stood on the sidewalk outside and watched the windows for movement. It didn't look like anybody was home yet.

What would he do if someone came out? Follow them? Hunt them? Did he have any right to do it? He was still holding the fang earring.

The back of his skull itched. He turned around to find that Bekah Riese had snuck up behind him.

Shock washed through him. He had a kind of sixth sense for werewolves, and they shouldn't have been able to sneak up on him. But Bekah barely registered. Werewolf-lite.

"You're a kopis, aren't you?" Bekah asked casually, as though they had been in the middle of a conversation. "One of those hunter things? My dad told me all about you guys."

Never talk to them when they're human, or they'll trick you. You'll get confused and sympathetic. That was what his mom always said.

She was probably right. Last time he talked to a werewolf, he ended up dating her.

Seth hadn't brought a gun, so he felt strangely exposed outside their house. He took his hands from his pockets and clenched them into fists, prepared for a fight.

Her gold eyes flicked to his hands and then back to his face. Her mouth turned down at the corners. She looked worried or scared. Maybe both.

She took a deep breath, visibly bracing herself.

"I saw you take copies of our school records off the secretary's desk while he was talking to someone. You're studying us, aren't you? We've been studying you, too. You, your brother, and Rylie. What would a hunter want with a werewolf?"

"None of your business," he said.

"Please don't hurt her."

Seth almost dropped his guard. That was a funny request, coming from a murderer. "I would never hurt Rylie."

"We're going to help her. That's why we came here, so we're keeping an eye on her." She clutched her necklace in both hands. "If anything happens to Rylie..." She straightened herself, pushing her shoulders back. "You and Abel will answer for it."

"She doesn't need help from your type."

Her head tilted as she studied him. "Oh no. You don't know yet... do you?"

He backed toward the road to keep her in his sight.

"Know what?"

Bekah smiled. It was small and nervous, but definitely a smile. "You'll find out soon." She paused before adding, "You won't believe me, but I'm sorry. Really."

Seth kept edging backward. He didn't turn around until he got to the corner of the sidewalk.

When he glanced over his shoulder, Bekah was still in the yard, still waiting and watching him with sparkling yellow eyes.

He went around the corner and she disappeared from sight.

Seven

Just Like Wolves

Rylie insisted on cooking dinner for Gwyn that night. She felt miserable from crying too much, but her aunt looked even worse. "You need the iron," Rylie announced as she carried steak into the living room.

Gwyn gave her a shrewd look. "You're six kinds of helpful all of a sudden. Maybe I need to get a cold more often."

"Cooking is my chore. I'm not being weird or anything."

"I've got a bug, babe. Don't start carving my tombstone yet. I'll be better after dinner and sleep, and you can go back to being a useless teenager again."

"It's a deal," she said with a forced smile.

Rylie hovered in the kitchen while Gwyn ate, watching silently through the doorway. Her aunt had a coughing fit and had to set down the fork to catch her breath.

How long had that chest cold been hanging around? Maybe it wasn't a cold at all. She had an appointment with her doctor at the end of the month, but Rylie wished it was sooner.

She did the dishes before collapsing in bed, totally tired and completely unable to sleep. The night after a moon, she usually blacked out for at least twelve hours. But her mind wouldn't shut up. She kept imagining Gwyn dead in the fields with Isaiah Branson's injuries.

Rylie held up her hand, watching the light on her ceiling through her fingers.

She had grown claws when she smelled Bekah in class. What would have happened if she hadn't stopped it? Would the rest of her body have changed, too?

Just because she hadn't done it before didn't mean it was impossible. Bekah did it. The thought of changing at will held no temptation for her. She didn't like transforming on the moons, so why would she do it willingly at other times?

But it wasn't painful or bloody for Bekah, was it?

Rylie buried her face into her pillow with a groan. "Stop thinking," she mumbled.

It was too late to banish the mental image of seeing Bekah trot away in wolf form. No blood. No screaming.

That kind of control wasn't exactly a cure, but it was almost as good.

Something tapped outside.

She went rigid. It was rhythmic and sharp, like metal drumming against glass.

Rylie got out of bed and peeked through the curtains. Abel's ugly, twisted face stared at her from the other side. "What is wrong with you?" she hissed, opening the window a crack.

"Are you sleeping?"

"It's night and this is my bedroom! What do you think I'm doing?" It occurred to her that she was wearing pajamas, and she folded her arms over her chest as she tried not to blush.

"Come on, let's go hunting," he said.

"Now?"

Abel grunted. "Yes, *now*. Hurry up."

He vanished. Rylie gaped at the spot he had been standing. "No," she said, even though he was gone. "This is stupid. I'm not doing it."

She found herself pulling a pair of Gwyn's jeans over her shorts anyway. By the time she added a jacket, gloves, and hat, she was sweltering and eager to get outside.

Abel waited by the truck. It must have been a million degrees below freezing, but he didn't have a jacket. He looked exhilarated and out of breath, and Rylie could see how handsome he might have been with his scars hidden by shadow.

He snorted when he saw her. "Nice. You look like a marshmallow."

"You look like you're going to die of hypothermia." Rylie wrinkled her nose. "Where's Seth?"

"Probably doing homework or being virtuous or something. I don't know, what am I? His babysitter?" He blew a breath out of his lips, and it fogged the air around him. "Forget Seth. How do you think you're going to run dressed like that?"

The question shocked her into dropping her earmuffs. "I'm not running anywhere!"

"You can't smell stuff from inside a truck."

Rylie was tired enough that it took several seconds for her to piece together his meaning. He wanted to run. He wanted to smell. He wanted to *hunt*—not with guns, but like wolves.

"You're crazy," she said flatly.

"Human Rylie is thinking too much right now. Where's wolf Rylie?" He glared into her eyes like he would be able to see the werewolf on the other side, and she gritted her teeth, refusing to back down.

"Wolf Rylie doesn't want to play with you either. We both think you're a jerk!"

She spun to stomp back inside.

Something clicked behind her.

It was a distinctive sound, and after the last few months, *way* too familiar. She looked over her shoulder to see Abel pull back the bolt on a rifle. It was pointed at her.

Stillness settled over her as the world came into sharp focus. She saw the way his hands were braced on the metal and the pulse in his throat and felt no fear.

Her lip curled.

"That's better," Abel said.

She circled him, and he tracked the rifle along her path. Rylie angled so she could duck behind the truck if he squeezed the trigger, but a whiff of something meaty blew past her.

A skinned rabbit had been left in the truck bed.

The wolf swelled to life as the odors and sounds of the ranch came rushing around her. She could smell the livestock and hear the rustling of animals in their shelters.

None of that mattered. There were more important smells. Other wolves.

"You want to get them, don't you?" he asked, voice low.

Rylie trotted down the hill without speaking. The trail of the wolves was old, but it grew stronger by the road.

Abel followed. Distantly, she realized two things—first, that he was no longer armed, and second, that he didn't smell like fresh gunpowder. The rifle hadn't been loaded. She didn't care anymore.

She inspected the fence at the highway junction. One of the wolves had rubbed against it.

"They've been watching for awhile, haven't they?"

Abel's words annoyed her, though they made little sense. She shook to loosen a strange pressure against her body. Jacket. Gloves. What was she doing wearing such human things?

Pushing off her hat, she followed the scents across the road. Abel was right behind.

The motion of Rylie's legs and pumping arms made her human mind drift away. Too hot, too constricted, too slow. Rylie dropped her outerwear until she was in jeans and a tank top, then kept running untouched by cold.

They slipped through the night as shadows, darting from hill to hill with their noses to the wind and bodies low.

Time blurred. All she knew was the hunt.

The smells changed as they reached the edge of town. Images of pink skin came to mind. The wolves became man and walked with the humans. Strange. Her nose wrinkled.

"Watch it," Abel said, grabbing her arm before she darted into the street. Headlights sliced through the darkness as a car sluiced past.

She stared at him blankly. *Watch it.* She couldn't wrap her mind around the meaning.

"Jesus, you go under hard," he muttered, studying her face. "You're not in there at all, are you?"

Too many words.

Abel tried to move ahead, but she reached out for him, digging claws into his upper arm. He swatted her hand away. "Let go."

She backhanded him. His head snapped back, and he staggered.

Rylie didn't follow Abel. He followed *her.*

When he came up, he looked furious. He wiped blood off his upper lip with his hand. But when he stalked toward her, she gave a warning growl, and he froze. He needed to know his place.

They stared each other down, and after a moment, he dropped his gaze. Good.

Leading the way through town, she didn't watch to make sure he stayed behind her like he was supposed to. She didn't have to.

Rylie and Abel stayed along the fringes of civilization, even though few people were outside on such a cold night. The scent of wolf-as-man became beastly again on the other side of town.

They sped along the highway, and the tracks split a mile down the road. Each was fresh and belonged to different wolves.

She circled the junction to evaluate both paths. The wolf that followed the highway was weaker. Its smell was tainted by something strange and sickly. They could take that one and go back for the other.

Rylie led Abel on, getting more excited as the smells strengthened. It wasn't long before they came upon another group of houses completely unlike the farms. These ones were surrounded by gates and gardens and icy fountains with a manmade lake in the center.

The fence was no challenge to climb. When they dropped to the other side, she knew they had found the wolf.

The lust for the hunt abruptly died.

Rylie knew that house. She recognized the fancy gate, all those cars, and the neatly-manicured bushes, even underneath the snow. She had wasted a lot of hours in the basement while her friends played video games. She could smell the bong from outside.

"Stop," she said when Abel moved forward. Forcing her tongue and lips to make sounds was harder than it should have been. "We can't go in there."

"Why? One of them is inside."

Rylie shut her eyes, shook her head, and tried to focus on human thoughts and feelings.

This is where Tate lives. My friends are playing games right now.

She realized belatedly that she was standing knee-deep in a snowdrift. Her shoulders were so cold she couldn't feel them. Her face burned with the slap of wind.

"What are we doing?" she asked, hugging herself. Her brain felt thick and fuzzy. "This is insane!" She rubbed her upper arms, trying to bring heat into them.

"It's too late to go back," Abel said. "We can finish this!"

"How? With your hands?"

He drew a knife from the back of his belt. It was wrapped in a plastic bag and sheathed in leather, but she could see a hint of silver metal.

"Yeah," he said. "With my hands."

She snarled. "Put that away!"

"If we don't do something now, the werewolf could kill one of these rich punks. You know that, right?"

Rylie punched the buzzer by the front gate. Abel nearly jumped out of his skin. "What are you *doing*?" He dragged her behind a bush flocked with ice and a good three inches of snow.

She shoved him. His back smacked into the brick wall.

"Don't touch me!"

"If that thing is living here—"

"It's not. Shut up." She cast a sideways look at the knife. "And I told you to put that away!"

It took a long time for anyone to respond to the buzzer, and in the meantime, Rylie danced from foot to foot to keep warm. Then something rustled over the speaker, and a sluggish voice asked, "What?"

"Requesting permission to enter the Tate Zone," she said through chattering teeth. Abel gaped at her.

Tate laughed. He was joined by at least three other voices. She thought she heard aliens getting shot on TV. "Is this Rylie? What are you doing outside in the middle of the night?"

"It's hard to explain, but I am *so* cold. Open the gate." It immediately unlocked with a buzz. Abel didn't move. "Come on. Seth would be annoyed if I let you freeze to death."

He followed reluctantly. Tate greeted them at the door.

"Dude, what the heck? You look like a freaking ice cube." He was in pajama pants and his hair stuck up in the back. He didn't look like he belonged among chandeliers or marble fixtures at all. His eyes widened when he spotted Abel. "Whoa. Who chewed your face?"

A growl rose in Abel's throat, and Rylie stepped between them. "This is Seth's brother. His car broke down and I forgot my phone," she said. "We had to walk here. Can we get a ride back to the ranch?"

Tate blinked. "Oh. Yeah, sure, let me tell the guys."

They waited upstairs while he went back into the basement, which was a horrible, stinking bachelor pad. She thought she might get a contact high when the door swung open.

But weed wasn't the only stench. She closed her eyes and took deep breaths.

The other wolf was downstairs.

Abel's upper lip pulled back to bare his teeth. He eyed the stairs. "Don't even think about it," she said. "Someone could get hurt."

He grinned. "That's the point."

"No. Do you hear me?"

Tate's friends followed him into the entryway. He pulled baggy jeans over his boxers, stuffing his hands down the sides to smooth them out. Rylie gave a little wave to the other guys, who went to the same school, but then she saw an unfamiliar face in the back.

He had the same honey-blond hair and sharp nose as Bekah. There was a silver stud in his left ear marked with a star.

Levi. It had to be.

"Don't even think about beating the boss until I'm back," Tate said, jabbing a finger at Patrick while John ambled toward the kitchen. They all smelled like potato chip grease and frozen pizza.

Patrick snorted. "Yeah, okay, whatever. Hey, Rylie."

She didn't hear him. Her eyes met Levi's. He looked surprised to see her, but not angry. It wasn't until he turned to Abel that a spark of challenge flashed through his gaze.

Rylie grabbed Abel's arm. She wasn't sure if it was to keep him from jumping on Levi, or to stop herself.

Tate didn't notice the sudden tension. "Want to borrow one of my mom's jackets?"

She caught onto the conversation and shook her head.

"I just want to go home."

"Cool," he said. "Come on, the garage is downstairs."

Tate regaled Rylie with stories of Dark Crash Exodus as he drove them home, punctuating it with words like "epic" and "awesome." She smiled and nodded along. Abel lurked in the backseat of the BMW like an angry shadow.

"Need someone to call a tow truck for your car, man?" Tate asked, pausing in the middle of his story to glance at Abel in the rearview mirror.

"We'll take care of it. Thanks," Rylie said.

He dropped them off and left again. Abel and Rylie sat on the front step of the house without talking.

She was too embarrassed to go inside, like she had done something shameful—even though nothing happened. She hadn't spoken to Levi Riese, much less tried to kill him. But she felt ashamed and dirty.

After working so hard to keep her wolf under control, all it took to get her mind shifting between moons was a dead rabbit and a gun with no bullets.

"Don't tell Seth," Abel said.

Rylie barked out a laugh. "I don't even know what I'm not going to tell him. That you're hunting behind his back? Or that you're hunting more like a werewolf than a human?"

"Any of it. Don't tell him."

They stared at each other silently. It was a moment they had shared too often over the last few weeks—a wordless exchange where they evaluated each other, as though trying to decide who was alpha.

Rylie spoke first this time. "You're supposed to be cured. Maybe if you tell Seth—"

He got to his feet. Abel was almost a foot taller than Rylie when they were both standing, so when she was sitting, he cut an imposing figure. "Don't forget I'm still a hunter, and you're still a werewolf."

"That threat doesn't mean anything anymore. If you were going to kill me, you would have already done it." He spun and jumped in the Chevelle. Before he could shut the door, Rylie's mouth opened again. She didn't mean to say what she was thinking, but she did. "I love Seth."

He stopped. "So?"

"So that means you might be my brother someday. If something is wrong with you, we can figure it out. All three of us. Together."

Abel slammed his door. The Chevelle's engine roared to life, and he tore down the hill.

Rylie's heart ached as she watched him go.

Eight

The Talk

When Rylie finally slept, she might as well have died for all that she was aware of the outside world. Her eyes shut as soon as she touched the pillow. Overwhelming darkness consumed her.

Dreams flickered at the edges of her mind. She had four legs and a mouth filled with blood.

Was it hers? Or did it belong to a fawn in a distant forest that had been dead for months?

A hand touched her. She jolted to consciousness, and for an instant, she thought Abel was sitting on the edge of her bed. She was so angry to see him that she almost snapped. Her lip peeled back with a growl.

But both sides of his face were whole and unscarred.

"Oh my God, Seth." She flopped back onto the bed. "Don't scare me like that!"

"Sorry." He bent to kiss her, but Rylie dragged her pillow over her face. Her morning breath could have scared any number of vicious werewolves away.

"How did you get in?" she mumbled into the pillowcase.

"The door. How else?"

Seth tried to uncover her head, but she clamped her hands tight on the pillow.

"Did you break the lock?"

He laughed. "Gwyn let me in. It's almost eight."

So she had slept in. She never slept in past five anymore. But Abel's little "hunt" meant she had gotten less than four hours of sleep, and trying to open her eyes made it feel like her eyelids were being dragged off her face.

Seth finally wrenched the pillow out of her arms, threw it across the room, and pounced. Rylie shrieked.

He pinned her to the bed, his hands pressing her wrists against the mattress, and then he was kissing her and Rylie had no idea who or what she was. He tasted warm and delicious with a hint of sugar. He'd already been into the energy drinks and protein bars. Breakfast of champions.

"Your breath is horrible," he said with a chuckle against her cheek.

She smacked her other pillow against the back of his head, hard enough to make their foreheads bump. "Shut your—"

His lips pressed against hers, defusing her annoyance in an instant. She wrapped her arms around his neck and relaxed against his body.

Rylie hadn't done a lot of kissing before—or any at all, actually, aside from Brent in the seventh grade, who had these horrible braces—but she was certain Seth was the best in the world. Every movement of his lips and tongue woke her up in places she hadn't felt before.

He pulled back so he could look in her eyes. His expression was dark and heated, like he was thinking about other things. Probably the same things as Rylie.

But before she could say anything, her door opened. Aunt Gwyn cleared her throat loudly.

Seth bolted upright. Rylie flattened out and hid her head behind his back. Her cheeks burned with heat. "Breakfast is ready," Gwyn said, her voice thick with amusement. She propped the door open before leaving again.

Rylie burrowed her head in the sheets. "I think the door is supposed to be a sign," Seth said.

"A sign that I'm going to die of humiliation," she said. Seth slipped off the bed and kneeled next to her so their faces were level. She peeked at him with one eye over the sheet.

He grinned. "I'm starving. Are you starving?"

Her stomach growled loud enough for both of them to hear it. He laughed and dragged her out of bed.

Rylie detoured to the bathroom to comb her hair and brush her teeth. They walked into the kitchen holding hands, but Rylie kept her eyes locked to the floor so she wouldn't have to look at anyone. Mercifully, Gwyn didn't ask any awkward questions.

As soon as they finished eating and rinsed off their plates, they were free to check on the cows. It looked like it wouldn't snow for a few days, so they were moving the herd out of the barn. Rylie had to break ice off the troughs so they would have something to drink other than snow.

Seth opened the barn doors and spread hay around the fields for them to graze on. Rylie sat back on the fence to watch him work. She couldn't actually approach the cows unless she felt like causing a stampede.

When was the last time she had seen Abel working around the cows? He was at the ranch every day, but she only saw him plowing snow or repairing fences. Was he avoiding the animals now, too?

She couldn't shake it off as paranoia. Not after what happened the night before.

He joined her on the fence when he finished. *Tell him about Abel. He has to know. Just tell him...*

"What are you going to do today?" she asked with an inward wince.

He wrapped his arm around her shoulders. "I'm going to check out some of the murder scenes, I think. The police have cleaned up by now, but maybe they missed something."

"Why don't we just go after Bekah and Levi?"

"Because..." Seth hesitated. "I don't know. We can't do anything until we're sure. We *have* to be sure."

Rylie watched her feet swing over the snow. "I guess."

"I'm going into the city today, too. I need to find a place that rents tuxedos."

"Huh?"

"Well, you know. For the Winter Ball."

Her heart skipped a beat, and she tilted her head back to look at him. "Did you hear they changed the date to the twenty-third? The new moon?"

"You've been doing really good on the days before you change. The dance is pretty early. I don't think it will be a problem, if you still want to go."

"You haven't even asked me," Rylie said.

Seth's arm tightened. "I didn't think I had to ask."

She pushed him away. "So what, you assumed you'd show up before the dance and I'd magically be ready to go? I need warning to get beautiful."

"You always look beautiful," he said, but she could tell he was just trying to dodge trouble. Seth moved toward her again and she hopped off the fence. "I'm sorry, okay? I didn't think it'd make you mad. Want to go to the Winter Ball?"

"Well, *now* I don't."

"Rylie..."

"I might be a werewolf, but I'm still a—a modern woman," she said, trying to summon up the same amount of dignity her therapist had when she said it. "I'm not going to go just because you snap your fingers at me."

"So you're mad I didn't ask, but now that I did, you're mad about that too?"

"Yes, but... no." She folded her arms. "You have to ask me the right way."

Seth dropped to his feet. "Okay, tell you what: You figure out how you want to be asked—if you want to be asked at all—and let me know if I should rent a tux or not. I'm going to get moving."

He gave an exaggerated sigh as he walked away, and she felt a little guilty. He was right. How did she expect him to ask her out? Seth almost made it back to his car before she called to him. "Hey!" she shouted. He turned around. "Do you want to go to the Winter Ball with me?"

"I'll think about it!" he yelled back.

Rylie was still grinning stupidly when she returned to the ranch house. She all but floated as she hung the rest of the Christmas lights. All thoughts of Abel had vanished. Her brain was stuck with Seth, and kissing in bed that morning, and the Winter Ball.

The dance was at a venue in the city. Rylie had heard some of the senior girls talking about getting hotel rooms to stay overnight with their boyfriends. Seth was a senior, too. She wondered if he'd want a room if she wasn't becoming a werewolf that night.

Rylie stared at herself in the mirror over the fireplace, and gold eyes stared back. A thrill shot through her stomach.

She was sixteen now—practically an adult. A lot of her guy friends back home had been having sex since they were fourteen or fifteen. Tyler even hooked up when he was thirteen, which had to be some kind of record. He sure bragged about it enough.

But she couldn't get excited about the prospect of a romantic evening. Seth and Rylie would definitely have a long night together, but they wouldn't enjoy it. He'd have to chase her all over the wilderness while she ate rabbits and picked fights with coyotes.

It wasn't exactly the most romantic thing she could imagine.

Gwyn appeared behind her reflection, and Rylie's cheeks flamed with heat. She jumped off the chair, feeling as embarrassed as though her thoughts were imprinted on her forehead.

"Are you busy?" Gwyn asked.

She picked at a box of decorations. "Oh yeah. Really busy."

"Want help?"

"I was actually going to do some homework and go into town. I need to buy a dress. Do you want me to get anything while I'm there?"

"We could use groceries. I'll give you a list," Gwyn said. Rylie could feel eyes burning on the back of her neck. "But we need to talk, babe."

Oh God.

"When you go into town today—anytime you're in town at all, actually—I don't want you at Abel and Seth's apartment. I know you've been over a couple of times. Should have told you sooner, I guess."

Rylie spluttered. "What? They're over here all the time."

"There's no adults there—and no, Abel doesn't count. There's more to adulthood than being over eighteen." Rylie opened her mouth to protest, but Gwyn cut her off with a slash of her hand. "They're good boys. Our doors will always be open to them. But you can't go over there, and you can't have Seth in your room. That's the rule."

"But that's stupid!"

"I know." Gwyn heaved a sigh. "I remember being a teenager. You know so much more than I do. But you're only sixteen, Rylie. You're too young to have sex."

Rylie's mouth fell open. Maybe her aunt *was* psychic. "I wasn't—I'm not—" She smothered her face in her hands. "I'm going to crawl into the duck pond and die."

"Suit yourself."

"We're not—I mean, we haven't—it's not like... *ugh.* I don't want to talk about this."

"Sex is complicated, Rylie," Gwyn said. "Sure, you can wear condoms and mostly prevent pregnancy—"

Rylie threw her hands in the air. "I'm not listening to this!"

Her aunt chuckled. "You can't ignore me because it's embarrassing."

"I won't go to their apartment. Okay? Happy?"

"That's all I'm asking." Gwyn sank onto the couch with a sigh. "So why do you need a dress?"

Grateful for the change in subject, Rylie sat on the arm beside her. "The Winter Ball is coming up. Christmas Eve."

"Is that a school event?" she asked. Rylie nodded. "I'm fine with it so long as there are chaperones." She made a few notes on a piece of paper. "Here's what we need from the store. Take some cash with you, get something nice. Don't bother bringing back change. Whatever's on my desk is fair game."

"Okay. Thanks."

Rylie surrendered the box of decorations and headed back to her aunt's bedroom.

Most of the house was decorated in country casual, but Gwyn's room could only be described as a "boudoir." Everything was dark wood, her sheets were crimson silk, and there was a weird velvet painting of a horse over the headboard.

Gwyn didn't trust banks, so she kept most of her money stuck in weird places around her desk. Rylie took a wad of cash out of the pen cup and hesitated before leaving again.

There were a lot of yellow pill bottles strewn around the room. It seemed like they were multiplying. Rylie worried her lower lip between her teeth. She didn't like seeing so many pills—it meant things weren't getting better. Stranger still, there was concealer in a dozen different shades on her bedside table, like Gwyn was trying to figure out what worked best.

She went back to the living room before she could see anything else strange and worrying.

Gwyn met her at the door, watching as Rylie put on boots and a jacket with a little smile.

"I remember when you were barely taller than my goats."

Rylie rolled her eyes. "Don't get all mushy on me."

"I wouldn't dream of it. Remember the spices. They're listed on the back."

They hugged, and Rylie took the opportunity to sneak a close look at Gwyn's face. She *was* wearing a lot of makeup. It looked like she was covering sores around her mouth. How hadn't Rylie noticed?

"I love you," she said impulsively. They weren't usually affectionate, but it came out before she could stop herself. "Even when you're embarrassing."

Gwyn ruffled her hair. "Drive safe, pumpkin."

It was the nickname Rylie's dad used to call her before he died of a heart attack, and it made her eyes burn to hear it coming from her aunt. Nobody had called her pumpkin in months.

She made it all the way to the truck before starting to cry.

Nine

In a Dark Alley

Long nights made the days fly by. Rylie passed out every night with the sunset and woke up twelve hours later feeling like she hadn't slept at all, dragging herself through chores and another day of school with heavy limbs.

Seth spent most of his breaks studying in the library or with the team, so Rylie tried to hang out with Tate instead. But Levi seemed to have become his new best friend. He didn't confront her or anything, but he was always around, thumbing that silver star on his earlobe and staring. Rylie couldn't stand his smell. It got bad enough that if she saw Tate approaching, she would turn around and head in the opposite direction instead.

"What's bugging you?" Tate asked in class one day.

She forced a casual shrug. Levi wasn't there, but his smell was all over Tate's hair and clothes. "It's not you. It's just..."

"Levi."

"Yeah." She smiled sheepishly.

Tate chucked her in the shoulder. "He's cool, but you're still my best bro. And the weirdest. Okay?"

"Okay," she said.

His reassurances didn't do anything to calm Rylie. In fact, it only made her worry more. She had no idea what a werewolf wanted with her friend, but she had a feeling it wasn't good.

Seth and Abel weren't the only ones who could investigate. And she didn't need their permission to hunt.

Rylie sneaked into her geography teacher's classroom while he was at lunch. She logged onto his computer using the password on a sticky note under his keyboard.

The student records were accessible through an icon on the desktop shaped like a door. She resisted the urge to check her grades and loaded Levi's records instead. Everything was there—his history of athletic extracurriculars, his perfect grades, and a list of every school he attended.

She emailed them to herself and jotted down Levi's address before logging out.

"What are you doing in here?" asked her teacher, entering with a lunch bag under one arm and a mouthful of tuna sandwich pouching his right cheek. It smelled horrible and stale.

"I thought I left my phone in here," she said.

He watched her leave with a suspicious look, but she hurried down the hall before he could ask more questions.

She felt jittery for the rest of the day, like someone would find out what she had done. She didn't care if the school caught her—what would one more red mark on her record mean anyway?—but feared what Bekah and Levi might do.

Fortunately, the afternoon passed uneventfully. Seth had practice after school and Tate drove off with Levi, leaving Rylie a whole boring evening on her own.

She turned on her phone to find a message from the tailor saying her dress was ready. Rylie left her car at the high school and wandered downtown, yawning and stretching. Her entire body was sore. Rylie didn't think she would ever sleep well again.

It was a sunny day, and the streets had been plowed, leaving the pavement damp and steaming. The little bell over the door jingled when Rylie walked into the tailor's.

He grinned when he recognized her. "You're going to love this."

They went into the back room. Her dress hung in a curtained room next to a full length mirror, and it was so big that she needed help getting it over her head.

The tailor laced the hooks up the back and then bustled around to double check his measurements. She stared at herself in the mirror with awe. She couldn't wait to see Seth's reaction. "It's perfect," she said. "This is great. Thank you so much."

"It's better than perfect," he said with a wink.

Rylie had already paid for the dress at the fitting, so she only had to take it home. He zipped it up in a bag and she carried it slung over her shoulder. It was bulky, but not heavy. Of course, nothing was too heavy for her anymore. She probably could have carried a car over her shoulder if it hadn't been such an awkward shape.

The wind shifted, and a whiff of something meaty caught her attention as she ambled down the road. She stopped and sniffed.

Something smelled amazing. It wasn't dinnertime yet, but she was suddenly hungry. She checked the time. Gwyn wouldn't mind if she was a few more minutes late.

She tracked the smell with her nose to the breeze, keeping an eye out for whatever restaurant was venting such a sweet smell. She hadn't heard about a new restaurant opening. It was a big deal whenever something opened in town—the lone Starbucks in the grocery store was still the talk of the town, and it had been built the year before.

Rylie stopped in front of a narrow alley between a diner and an antique shop.

Another sniff. That was definitely the source of the smell. But it wasn't coming from the buildings—it was coming from the trash.

Why would an alley smell so good? Maybe something was rotting in the Dumpster. *Gross*. One of the weirdest parts of becoming a werewolf was that everything smelled interesting, even things that should have been icky.

She couldn't resist the urge to find out what smelled so strongly. Rylie climbed over a pile of plowed snow and peered into the trash.

A leg was sticking out of the trash bags. A *human* leg.

She gasped and jerked back. Her foot slipped in the snow and she landed hard on her butt, scrambling back on all fours as if she could escape what she had seen. Her dress bag landed on damp sidewalk and she didn't even care.

Fumbling for her cell phone, she pressed the speed dial for Seth. It picked up on the third ring.

"What?"

"Seth! There's a body, someone's dead, it's in an alley—"

"Who is this? Rylie?"

The voice was too deep and gruff to belong to her boyfriend. She groaned. "What are you doing with this phone, Abel?"

"Seth forgot it at home. Who died? Where's the body?"

She bit her lower lip. She didn't want to see Abel—ever again, preferably.

"I'll just call the cops."

"Don't. We'll lose the chance to collect our own evidence. Tell me where you are."

Reluctantly, Rylie gave him directions to the alley. She didn't like having to wait near the body. It smelled delicious— oh my *God* it smelled good, and that was so horrible—but she was afraid it would vanish if she left.

Every time a car passed, she tried not to look nervous. It was hard to believe that everyone else couldn't smell it.

Abel showed up five minutes later. He brought a cheap digital camera, rubber gloves, and sandwich bags. Her stomach flipped at the sight of him.

"Don't tell me you're going to touch that thing," she said, feeling nauseous.

"Fine. I won't tell you."

Abel climbed into the Dumpster like it was a totally normal thing to do and started digging around. Shifting the trash made the smell waft toward her more strongly.

"It's just like the other ones," he said. "Her throat's been ripped out, but there's no other major injury."

"I don't want to know."

He gave a low whistle. "It's pretty bad."

"I said I don't want to know!"

The camera clicked as Abel took pictures from various angles. He took long enough that curiosity got the better of her, and she edged her way up the pile of snow to give a sideways peek at his shoulders over the rim of the Dumpster.

"Definitely just her throat." Abel jumped out and peeled off the gloves, dropping them in an empty sandwich bag. He had bits of hair and blood in the other ones. It looked like he had taken some kind of tissue sample.

"Oh my God," she whispered, covering her nose and mouth with her hands.

"You think this is bad? This is just the start." Abel grinned. How could he smile like that?

"We have to do something," Rylie said.

"We could have gotten that Levi kid the other night."

Maybe he was right. Maybe the woman would have survived if they had finished the job when they had the chance. Rylie could tell her thoughts were showing on her face because Abel gave a grim nod.

"What happens next?" she asked.

He smirked at her. That lopsided smile looked like Seth's, but so much more sadistic. If Rylie had still been dreaming, she thought his smile would show up in her nightmares.

"You can call the police if you want. I'm taking these home to do a little more research." He wiggled one of the bags at her.

Something slimy and red slid around the inside of it. "Have to put the evidence on ice."

That was too much for Rylie to handle. The sour taste of bile stung her throat.

Abel's laugh echoed behind her as she fell to all fours and threw up on the sidewalk.

Ten

Levi

Seth struggled with self-doubt.

He had done more research on the Riese siblings. He tracked their history back for two years, and found nothing that indicated they were killers. But a big chunk of time was missing. It was like the records for two years had been completely removed.

That was the kind of thing Seth's mom looked for when searching for damning evidence surrounding a werewolf, but he didn't know what to do with it.

For the first time since she left, Seth wished his mother was there so they could talk about it. His dad had been a werewolf expert, but he wasn't sure if they ever killed teenage werewolves. Levi was his age. Bekah was a little younger. Hunting them seemed… wrong.

He knew Bekah Riese was waiting for him to make a move. She was always watching when Seth was with Rylie at school. It made Seth feel like he was the one being hunted instead of doing the hunting for once.

When Seth went for lunchtime practice in the gym on Wednesday, it was no surprise to find Levi warming up with the team. But he *was* surprised to see Rylie waiting for him, too.

She was at the top of the stands with her knapsack by her side and her hair in thick braids like Gwyn's.

He waved at her. She gave him a weak smile.

Seth changed in the locker room and came out to find the guys shooting hoops. There wasn't enough time for an organized game, but they dribbled the ball up the court and back again, elbowing each other and dodging and laughing.

The ball flew at Seth, and he caught it. He was surprised to see Levi had thrown it.

"You going to play?" he asked.

A group of girls on the bottom row of bleachers giggled and sighed. Rylie had gone pale.

"You're on," Seth said.

A skirmish between the two city guys was too exciting to miss. The other athletes backed up with hoots and cheers. He couldn't tell if they were cheering more for him or Levi.

He bounced the ball a couple times to loosen his shoulders, then went for the hoop.

Levi jumped in front of him. Seth twisted, guarding the ball with his body, and made a wide turn so he could run toward the end of the court.

A hand shot in front of him, knocking the ball out of the way.

People yelled as Levi made a fast lap around the gym. Seth blinked. He'd moved too fast to be seen, using his supernatural werewolf speed to steal the ball.

"Cheating?" he muttered under his breath.

Levi's eyes glinted. "I'm not holding back. Are you?"

Rylie stared hungrily from the top of the bleachers as Seth took a deep breath, opening up all those special senses that made him the "legendary hunter" Bekah had called him. He ignored it most of the time. He didn't like to show off.

But now he narrowed his entire focus on Levi and those piercing golden eyes.

The werewolf tried to fake him out by feinting to one side and then darting in the other direction, but Seth saw the move coming. He stole the ball and bolted.

Levi was a blur as he darted in the way. Seth twisted and changed direction.

The ball was stolen. Seth took it back a half second later.

Girls screamed as Seth dribbled across the court. His heart pounded in his ears. He just needed to get across, and then he would be in the clear, and—

Levi flew past him. The ball was gone.

He slam-dunked and hung off the rim. The onlookers roared, stomping their feet and clapping, and Seth felt numb in the center of the court. Levi dropped to his feet, folded his arms across his chest, and stared at him in challenge.

Levi was strong and fast—and definitely better at basketball.

But was he deadlier?

He imagined squeezing his finger on the trigger of his gun and the blood fountaining down Levi Riese's triumphant expression. He could imagine himself kneeling by the body, snapping off a tooth, and making a matching earring.

Rylie stood in the bleachers, chewing on her thumbnail. She was whiter than the snow outside.

"Rematch?" Levi asked, tossing the ball at him. Seth let it bounce past him.

Soon. Very soon.

He went back into the locker room without responding.

Rylie's wolf was hungry for Levi Riese.

She shouldn't have watched them playing basketball. Her skin was hot, her hands were shaking, and all she could think about was the taste of blood. Eating roast beef for lunch did nothing. She was *starving*.

The address for the Riese house was in her pocket. Abel was right. They had to do something now—before anyone else got hurt.

So she ditched her last class and went to find their den.

The house Bekah and Levi lived in looked plain from the outside. Rylie had seen it a hundred times when she wandered around town and hadn't given it much thought.

Nobody was home. The fresh snow was undisturbed. Rylie peeked in the front windows, hands cupped around her face.

What did she think the living room of a couple murderous werewolves should look like? It seemed way too normal. They had a nice TV. Their furniture was leather, and there was a menorah on the table by the window. But she didn't see any meat hooks, bloody handprints, or the other kinds of icky things she expected murderers to have.

"Took you long enough."

Rylie whirled, clutching her knapsack to her chest. Levi stood behind her with a knitted hat pulled down to his eyebrows. The wolf's thoughts cascaded underneath hers in a torrential river of inarticulate desires: violence and hunger and the need to defend her territory.

"It's you," she growled.

"And Tate."

It was only then that she noticed the black BMW on the street. The wolf immediately silenced.

She straightened her back. "We have to talk, you and me, whether you like it or not. We've got to take care of this now."

"Take care of what?" Tate asked, bounding up the path.

Rylie plastered a smile on her face. "Hi."

"I forgot to tell you I invited Rylie to pizza," Levi said. "Come on, guys."

His back was turned to her while he unlocked the door. Rylie considered attacking, but Tate was *right there*, cupping his hands around a joint as he lit up. The time wasn't right. She had to wait.

They went inside, and Rylie was surrounded by the stench of other wolves. She had to brace herself on the back of the couch before she fell over.

Levi slouched into the kitchen as Tate flopped on the sofa. He took a long drag, holding it in for a few seconds before blowing out a thick cloud. "I didn't know you and Levi are friends," he said in a gravelly voice.

She was still smiling like an idiot. "We're not—I mean—I'm just getting to know him."

"Cool. I thought you hated him." Tate took another puff. "That's cool."

Wasn't everything cool with Tate? She wondered if he would be so relaxed if he knew what his new friend did on the full moon.

Levi came out of the kitchen, turned on the TV, and lifted Tate's legs so he could sit underneath them on the sofa. They looked... cozy. And they both ignored her completely as they shared the joint.

Taking deep, measured breaths (which made her a little light-headed from the smoke), Rylie forced herself to sit on the edge of a chair and keep smiling.

"So what are you guys up to?" she asked.

"Chilling for now," Levi said. "But we're going to pick up our tuxes for the ball later."

She blinked. "You're both going?" Bloodthirsty werewolves in formalwear fit her expectations as much as a nice middle class werewolf den. "Who are you two taking?"

Tate laughed and offered her the joint like usual, even though she always refused. "I'm taking Levi."

She had to process that for a good long minute before the meaning sunk in. "You're... taking... Levi?"

"That's what I said."

"You mean on a date," she said.

Tate was dating Levi.

Her best friend was dating a werewolf.

Everything Rylie thought she knew about Tate and Levi was destroyed. Her assumptions were completely wasted—like "blown away in a nuclear holocaust" wasted. She stood and paced in a circle even though she knew it made her look like a spazz.

"Dude," Tate said. "Chill."

"I'm chill. I'm really chill. I couldn't be chillier if I jumped in a freezer." She spun on Levi. "I'm hungry. Do you have anything to eat?"

He took a hint and went back into the kitchen. Rylie crouched by Tate.

"You cannot date him," she whispered urgently. When he moved to take another drag of his joint, she seized his wrist. His eyes widened at the strength of her grip. "Seriously, Tate, listen to me. *You cannot date Levi Riese.*"

He sneered. "I thought you'd be cool with it. You're not one of these tiny-brained, inbred farmers. Seriously, Rylie?"

"What? No, I don't mean it like that. You just don't know Levi! He's dangerous!"

"And you two are like total best friends?"

"That's the problem," she said. "You shouldn't—"

Levi interrupted them by returning with a plate of reheated pizza. "Cheese and oregano for Tate," he said, setting down one plate, "and all meat for Rylie. I know it's your favorite."

She glared.

Rylie didn't want to leave them alone, so she sat through their afternoon snack. The all meat really was her favorite. She ended up picking off the toppings and leaving the rest. To her surprise, Levi ate the whole pizza—crust, sauce, and everything. Rylie hadn't thought werewolves ate bread and liked it.

"I'll clean up," she said, leaping to her feet when she finished.

"There's not a lot of—"

She gritted her teeth as she grinned. "I'd be happy to do it."

Rylie took the dishes to the kitchen. The instant the door swung shut, she dropped them on the counter and started searching. She wasn't sure what she expected to find. A murder weapon? Evil plans?

The kitchen was as normal as the living room. They had marble countertops and ceramic flooring. There was a picture of an older woman hugging Levi and Bekah as they all laughed. A giant wooden pentacle hung on the opposite wall, decorated with garland and holly, though it didn't look like a holiday decoration.

Rylie recoiled to see it. She grew up going to church and had a pretty healthy relationship with God—until He decided to "bless" her with a werewolf bite, anyway. The five-pointed star made her queasy.

Were they Satanists? Was that why they wore those necklaces?

She shuffled through their drawers, but the only weird thing she found were candles. Not just tea lights, which Rylie used to decorate her bedroom, but big tapers in every color. They smelled like wax, herbs, and essential oils. More pentagrams had been carved into them. They gave her the creeps. She didn't touch them.

"We're heading out!" Tate shouted from the other room.

That was it. No more time to search.

She slammed the drawers shut and went back, wiping her hands on her jeans like they were wet from doing the dishes. "All done," she said brightly. Levi must have known what she was doing, but he didn't confront her.

"So are you coming with us to the city?" Tate asked, extinguishing the joint with the tips of his fingers.

"My aunt's expecting me. I better not."

She tried to think of something, *anything*, she could say to make the guys go separate ways. But nothing came to mind. Tate got in the BMW and started warming it up, and Rylie grabbed Levi's arm.

"What are you doing?" she hissed. "You can't date Tate! He's human!"

"You're dating a human. What makes you special?"

"Because he's—because I'm not—" Rylie floundered for words. "I'm not a killer!"

"We're all killers," Levi said. "But I'm not going to hurt Tate. He's safe with me. I'll take care of him."

"But—we have to—"

"Later. We'll talk. I swear."

All she could do was stand back on the driveway and watch them go, helpless and scared and a little confused.

What makes you special?

"But I'm not like you," Rylie whispered to the receding BMW.

Eleven

Visitor

Seth picked the lock on the coroner's office in twenty seconds flat.

He kept different locks in a bag under his bed and practiced picking them when he had a few extra minutes, and he had gotten good at it. But the coroner's office was no challenge. Nobody in such a small town bothered with security.

The door was open and he was inside before so much as a single car passed on the street.

Seth navigated the dark office without turning on his flashlight. His boots made the floorboards creak no matter how quietly he stepped, and every little noise made him jump. He pulled the curtains shut in the back office before turning on the coroner's computer.

The monitor's glow illuminated the room with stark shadows and burned his eyes. It was an old machine, and she had everything saved on the desktop. He started randomly clicking folders. It was all personal stuff—photos of the coroner's son and an impressive collection of MP3s.

"Where are the records?" he muttered as he searched through the file trees.

How hard could it be to find a coroner's information on police investigations? But there was nothing. It didn't even look like the computer connected to the internet.

His eyes traveled to a row of filing cabinets against the wall.

Seth turned off the monitor and opened the first cabinet. It was filled with manila folders arranged by date and case number.

"No way," he said with a disbelieving snort. Paper filing. Too weird.

All of the bodies that had been mauled in "animal attacks" were grouped together, so he grabbed the whole stack, sat at the desk, and kicked his feet up on the blotter. He read them using the light from his cell phone.

Deciphering the coroner's handwriting was the hardest part. It took him a good minute of squinting to recognize Isaiah Branson's name and figure out the date.

Surprise washed over him. There had been other bodies before the farmer.

The files went back for weeks. Branson was the fourth to die, though it looked like the police hadn't connected them until the death of the librarian at Turner's Crossing. There had been another three deaths since then, including the one Abel reported finding in an alley downtown.

Seven bodies. Two months.

Seth flipped through the school records he had downloaded to his phone. Two months before, Levi and Bekah Riese had still been enrolled in a school at Los Angeles.

He turned on the desk lamp and snapped pictures of the case files. He made sure to get names, dates, and addresses, as well as the autopsy photos. They were hard to look at.

When Seth killed werewolves, they stayed furry—he hadn't seen many dead people before.

He started to forward the images to Abel, but paused before hitting send.

If Bekah and Levi weren't the murderers... then who had done it?

A horrible idea occurred to Seth—so terrible he didn't want to consider it. But once it came to him, it lodged in his mind and began growing.

Who had come to town two months before? Who could be strong enough, brutal enough, to murder innocent people?

He turned off his phone, replaced the files, and snuck out the office the way he came in. It was snowing again. The world was quiet and still.

When he got home, he found Abel sleeping on his futon. He was so big that his feet and arms flopped off the sides. He had a sharpening stone and a giant knife with a serrated edge next to him. The blade was so big it might as well have been a sword.

How hard would it be to tear out someone's throat with a knife and make it look like a bite wound?

Abel stirred. One eye peeked open. "Why are you staring at me, you creepy little punk?"

"Stop being paranoid and go back to sleep." He took off his boots and sat down. His brother scrubbed his face and rolled over, giving a bleary blink at the clock on their satellite box.

"It's late. Where were you?"

"With Rylie."

Abel flopped onto his back. "What were you two doing?"

"None of your business," Seth said.

His brother snorted and threw a hand out, feeling blindly for the knife. He found it, sheathed it, and tucked it under his pillow. "Nice. You could have any cheerleader you wanted at school, and you're still with the werewolf."

He was trying to pick a fight, but Seth didn't feel like arguing. "What would you say if I told you that Bekah and Levi are innocent? Their school records say they were still in California when the first people died."

"I'd say school records are easy to fake."

That hadn't occurred to him. It didn't ease the tension at all. "I don't think they're the killers," Seth said. "They're immune to silver. Bekah said she wants to help Rylie. I think—I mean, I believe them. They're different."

Abel gave a long groan. "You're getting soft."

"Am I?"

He didn't respond. Seth squinted in the darkness. Abel's eyes were closed, and his chest rose and fell with slow, deep breaths. Asleep.

Seth stayed awake to watch his brother all night long.

Rylie woke up the next morning with a sticky mouth and a horrible headache. She didn't even look at herself as she scrubbed her teeth and spat red-stained toothpaste into the sink. Her eyelids felt like they were sticky with glue and every muscle ached. She didn't want to go to school.

The only thing that got her out of the house—aside from Gwyn's threatening death-glare—was the thought of seeing her boyfriend.

But Seth wasn't at school, and he didn't respond to her text messages.

It frustrated her to think of Seth and Abel hunting without her, but she couldn't go looking for them. Friday was therapy, as usual, and Gwyn would know if she skipped out on it.

The secretary set down her knitting long enough to tap the buzzer that alerted the therapist of a patient's arrival. "He's on a conference call right now," she said in a kindly voice when Rylie moved to go into the office. "You can sit out here and wait with me."

She dropped onto the waiting room couch. "How long do you think he'll be?"

"Not long at all."

Rylie crossed her legs at the ankles and tried not to fidget too much. Having to wait made irritation prick at the back of her neck. "So what's this guy's name?"

"Scott Whyte," said the secretary. "He's a psychologist from California. He looks a bit like an old movie star—Sean Connery or something." She giggled like she was a teenager instead of a gray-haired lady with a scarf covered in cats.

Scott Whyte.

The name filled her with dread. Why did that sound familiar?

Rylie suddenly wanted to run. It felt like the office had closed in on her like a cage. She was sure she had never met him before, and she couldn't bring a face to mind, but she *needed* to get away.

Abandoning her promise to Gwyn, she obeyed the urge in her gut that told her to flee.

But then the office door opened.

An unfamiliar man with a shock of white hair and a square jaw—just like an aging movie star who had put on thirty pounds—came through the doorway.

The wolf inside Rylie loosed a growl. She had to clap a hand over her mouth to keep from vocalizing it.

"You must be Rylie," Scott said. "Please, come in."

She didn't move. Why was the wolf so scared?

"I just remembered I have to do something," she said. It barely came out louder than a whisper. "Can I reschedule?"

"You're already here. Come on in and shut the door."

He went inside and sat at Janice's desk. Reluctantly, she followed, but stuck by the chessboard. She took a sniff. His smell was familiar.

"I can't stay long," she said.

He gestured to the chair in front of him. "You've got me for a whole hour. Sit, please. I've wanted to meet you for quite some time."

Scott Whyte's polo shirt gapped at the collar. She glimpsed a chain and smelled something unpleasant. Rylie realized, suddenly, that she knew what was on the end of that chain—the same star that Bekah and Levi wore.

"Werewolf," she snarled.

"Wait!" he said when she grabbed the doorknob. "We have to talk!"

Heat radiated from her bones, making her abs clench and fingers itch. Rylie didn't have to look down to know her fingernails were loosening again. She didn't even care.

"This is a trap," she said, lisping on the words around teeth that were growing long and sharp. She could imagine sinking her teeth into his throat all too clearly.

"No. This is a talk. Nothing more. Can we do that?" He stayed seated. When she didn't move, he went on. "Do you remember a woman named Rita Patterson?"

How could she forget? When Rylie tried to tell her aunt about the werewolf thing, Gwyn took her to a hospital for a psychiatric evaluation. Rita was the woman who analyzed her. She'd worn a silver star around her neck, too, and told her not to tell anyone else she was a werewolf.

Suddenly, she remembered where she had heard Scott Whyte's name before. "Rita tried to refer me to you. She said you were an expert in… my type of problems. But I didn't have a way to visit California. I didn't realize you're a…"

"I'm not a werewolf. I'm a priest in a large Wiccan coven based in Long Beach. Do you know what Wiccans are?" She shook her head. "You could call us 'witches' if you like. We don't have a church, but if we did, 'coven' would be the word for our congregation. You might think of me as a youth pastor. I specialize in young witches and werewolves. In fact, I have a pair of teens living with me that you should know by now."

"Levi and Bekah are your kids. I've been to your house."

"My wife and I adopted them. Their parents couldn't handle their… special needs."

Rylie felt dizzy and hot. She wished Seth was there. "What do you want from me?"

"Rita said a teen werewolf fell into her hospital, and she thought you needed our guidance. We've traveled all this way to help you, Rylie."

"And to kill people?"

"No," Scott said. "Absolutely not. Bekah and Levi have had problems, but they're good people. More importantly, they're in control." He leaned forward on the desk. "I can help you learn that kind of control."

She faltered. Her hand slipped off the doorknob. "You mean, you're the one that taught them to change on command?"

"They learned that on their own. I helped give them coping tools—and a few spells. You notice they wear silver? I enchanted their jewelry. It subdues the spirit of the wolf so they can control themselves."

The full implications of what he said sunk in. She felt light-headed.

"I can learn to change on command?"

"They still change on full and new moons, but they don't lose themselves like most werewolves."

"Does it hurt?" Rylie asked.

Scott steepled his fingers as he considered the question. "Most of the time... no. You've seen how good Bekah is at changing between moons—that's her unique talent. Levi struggles. But it doesn't hurt."

"What about on the moons?"

His expression was gentle. "That's a different situation."

Her budding hope was immediately crushed. *It will always hurt.* She bit the inside of her cheek so hard it bled, but it held back her tears. "What do I have to do to learn what they know?" Her voice shook despite herself.

"You have to come with me. My coven can help you."

"Let me talk to Seth," Rylie said. "He's a—um, he's my boyfriend. He's helping me now."

Scott pushed back his chair to stand. "That's something we need to discuss. Those brothers—those hunters—they're dangerous. Yes, I know what they are," he said upon seeing her shocked expression. "This invitation only extends to you. We need to get you out of here before they realize you're gone."

Leave Seth?

"No," Rylie whispered.

"It's okay," Scott said, stepping around his desk. "I'm here to help you."

A growl ripped from her throat. "Don't come near me!"

He froze.

Fury gripped her. Seth's voice filled her mind. *Deep breaths. Think about something nice.* But it was hard to focus on something *nice* when all she could do was focus on the pulsing vein in Scott's throat.

Rylie grabbed the doorknob. He moved to stop her, but she ignored him.

She made it halfway down the street before he called to her.

"Rylie!"

She kept running. If she had to smell Bekah on him one more time, she would completely lose it.

Levi was dating her best friend. Her new psychologist was some kind of witch. Those people were taking over her life when all Rylie wanted to do was survive.

Why couldn't they leave her alone?

She ran to Seth and Abel's apartment. The Chevelle was parked outside, but she shoved her way inside without knocking.

"Seth!"

But he wasn't there. Abel was polishing the parts of a gun while sitting on his futon. He didn't look surprised to see her. "What do you want?"

She stopped short, staring around at the walls.

The apartment had changed since her last visit. Newspaper articles were pinned to every wall. A giant map of the area, printed on multiple sheets of plain paper, hung over Seth's bed with color-coded pins stuck around town. A few banker's boxes were scattered around the floor, too.

Rylie realized she was gaping and shut her mouth. "What's going on here?"

"It's 'the process,'" Abel said, snorting. "My little man's more like our mom than he thinks."

"The process?"

"It's how we hunt." He gestured at the map with the muzzle of the pistol. "Those werewolf kids live at the house under the blue pin. Last I heard, he's trying to figure out where they den up during the moons."

A chill rolled down Rylie's spine. "They're living with a witch guy in a house outside town."

"Yeah. We know."

"You know?" she asked, eyes widening. "If you already knew, why didn't you tell me?"

Abel set down an oil rag, peered closely at the barrel of his gun, and grabbed a thin rod. "We don't have to tell you everything. Or anything at all. We were hunting a long time before you came around, and we'll do it after you're gone, too. We've seen witches before."

"I thought you only hunted werewolves."

He shrugged. "I'll hunt anything dangerous. It's fun."

She backed toward the door. "Maybe I should..." Rylie caught something red out the corner of her eye. She turned to see a bulletin board covered in photographs. Her brain pieced together the stark shapes—a foot, a garbage bag, a Dumpster.

Rylie clapped a hand over her mouth.

"It's worse in the pictures," Abel said from right behind her. She whirled. He was only inches away.

The wolf reacted to his presence with excitement. Anticipation. It wanted to hunt again. "Their dad insisted that Bekah and Levi didn't do it," she said, backing up until she hit the wall.

"He's lying. When did you talk to him?"

"A few minutes ago. My therapist is out of town, and he filled in for her."

"That's a heck of a coincidence," Abel said.

"No... it's not." She took a deep breath. "He offered to teach me control."

His eyes narrowed. He stepped forward, and there was nowhere else for Rylie to escape. "You don't need control," he said. "You need release."

The wolf loved the sound of that. A little too much, in fact.

She edged toward the door.

He didn't follow. He sat on the futon and picked up the oil rag again. "You better get home. Your aunt says you're not allowed to hang out here."

"What? She told you that?"

Abel looked like he had eaten something sour. Apparently, the idea of acting like a grown up didn't sit well with him. "She's right. Go away. I'll tell Seth you were here."

Twelve

Super Healing

Rylie tried not to think about witches, leaving Seth, or hunting as she drove home. She turned up the radio extra loud and focused on the slick road.

But nothing could push away the strange feeling that had settled over her since speaking to Scott.

It's always going to hurt.

She took a long, shuddering breath. "That's it," she announced to her reflection in the rearview mirror. "No more. Self-pity doesn't help anything."

Unsurprisingly, that didn't fix anything.

Gwyn wasn't in the house when she got home, which meant she was probably working with the cattle. Since Christmas was only three days away, Rylie took the chance to wrap gifts as a distraction. She hadn't bought much. She got Seth books to help him study for his exams and nice new boots for Gwyn. The big box was fun to wrap.

Once she finished, the house felt too empty. She didn't want to be alone with her thoughts.

Rylie dressed in warm clothes and headed out to the stable to find Butch. His stall was empty. Gwyn must have taken him instead of her normal horse.

She walked out to the pasture behind the barn. The cows had already worked their way through most of the hay Seth had put out with the tractor, so it looked like Gwyn was preparing to give them more to lead them back to the barn before it snowed heavily again.

The tractor sat in the middle of the field with a bale of hay in its prongs. Nobody was in the driver's seat.

A horse wandered up to Rylie, and she knew it had to be Butch before she could make out his face markings. The other horses were too scared of her wolf smell. But Butch was so old and slow that he wouldn't have run from a tiger if it jumped out of the bushes.

She caught his bridle and rubbed his nose.

"What are you doing out here saddled up and alone?"

He tossed his head and danced on his hooves. Rylie reined him in, climbed onto his back, and turned to head back the way he had come.

The breeze wafted the odor of sickness to Rylie's nose—a distinctive smell that was unpleasant to her as a human, and way too attractive for the wolf. It was touched with urine, too. But not a cow's urine.

Rylie crested the rise and saw a crumpled figure in the snow. Her heart stopped beating.

"Gwyn!"

She jumped off, ran to her aunt, and rolled Gwyn over to find her face blue. Her breathing was slow. Her eyelids barely fluttered at Rylie's touch.

"Jane?" Gwyn mumbled.

"I'm not Jane. I'm your niece," Rylie said. Jane used to be Gwyn's partner, but they had been separated for ten years. She bit back sudden tears. "Hey, don't pass out again. You have to stay awake. What happened?"

She responded with incoherent mumbles.

Rylie lifted her, and she was so light that her bones might have been replaced with marshmallow.

She tried to put her aunt in Butch's saddle, but Gwyn wouldn't sit upright, so she had to lay her across his back instead. Her thick braids dangled toward the ground.

The way back to the house never seemed to take so long before. Gwyn didn't wake up when she carried her into the house and removed her outerwear.

Her hat had fallen off somewhere. Rylie would need to find it. It was a really nice hat, and Gwyn wouldn't want it destroyed, maybe she should have gone back for it—but why was she worrying about the hat anyway?

Rylie set her on the couch before calling for help. She sat beside her on the floor as the man on the emergency line asked questions she couldn't answer.

What had Gwyn been doing when she collapsed? Was she coherent? Did she have any pain, or problems breathing?

"I don't know," she said, over and over again. "I don't know."

Time moved at a weird rate. She sat beside Gwyn for at least a hundred years. When the ambulance arrived, everything sped and blurred.

All of a sudden, she found herself in a chair in the hospital waiting room. She didn't remember the ride into town or her aunt getting admitted. She tried not to cry too loudly while the nurses worked on Gwyn. She kept worrying about the stupid hat and wondering if her dad's heart attack had been anything like this.

The hospital stunk of disinfectant and medication and sickness. She wished that she could turn off her sense of smell for a few minutes. Rylie didn't want to know about the dead body being moved two halls down, or that someone had vomited in the room beside Gwyn's.

All those sick people. All that prey waiting to be picked off.

She smothered her tears in her hands.

"Rylie!"

The sound of Seth's voice made Rylie go weak with relief. He hurried into the waiting room, and she somehow found the strength to stand up long enough to bury her face in his shoulder. "Thank you for coming," she whispered.

He kissed the top of her head and pressed his cheek to her hair. "What happened?"

"I don't know. I got home and I couldn't find Gwyn, and the horse was wandering around on its own, and then—I found her. She had collapsed and fallen or something. Nobody told me what's wrong. She just... collapsed."

"It's okay," he said, squeezing tighter. "It's okay."

Waiting to hear about her aunt's condition made Rylie not feel up to talking very much, but Seth waited with her anyway. She bit her fingernails until they bled, and then her hands warmed with her healing powers, and she started biting again.

After she destroyed her thumbnail three times in a row, Seth grabbed her fist.

"Don't do that."

She shook him off and paced the waiting room, stuffing her hands under her arms. "How long can it take to look at her? Why can't we go inside? Someone needs to tell me *something!*"

He didn't seem to hear her. He was staring at the TV. "Wait. Look at this."

Seth reached up to increase the volume.

"...Maria Sharp left behind two kids and a husband, who say her love of baking and talented hand with a woodcarving knife will be sorely missed." The news anchor had perfect hair, perfect teeth, and a perfectly sculpted sympathetic look. "Donations and gifts are being accepted at the Mill Street Baptist Church, where her family will be holding the memorial. In other news..."

"So what?" Rylie asked.

"You missed the headline," he said, his brow drawn low to shadow his eyes. "She was killed in the animal attacks."

She knew it was bad, very bad, and that there was something wrong about that news—beyond the fact someone had been killed—but she didn't care enough to puzzle it out. Who cared about some dead woman anyway?

"Oh no," she said flatly.

"I should have done something," Seth muttered. It was quiet enough that Rylie wasn't sure she was supposed to hear. "I should have been watching."

But people were still going in and out of Gwyn's door and she didn't care what he had to say. Rylie wanted to grab the nurses and force them to tell her what was wrong. She angled herself to peer in her aunt's door when it swung open again. The curtains were closed.

What was taking so long?

"Do you think Abel's been acting weird?" Seth asked.

"What?" She stretched on her toes to see over a doctor when he slipped around the curtain, but a nurse obscured her view. Rylie caught up with the conversation a moment later. "Abel... weird?" She still hadn't told Seth about their hunt. "I don't know what you're talking about."

"I've found nothing that points to Levi and Bekah being killers," Seth said, keeping his voice low and an eye on the hall. Nobody was close enough to hear their conversation. "In fact, people have been dying in these animal attacks for two months."

"Does that mean it's actually animals?" Rylie asked.

Tension radiated from his shoulders. He suddenly wouldn't look at her. "Maybe. I don't know. I don't have any leads."

His smell changed. Was he lying?

Gwyn's door opened again, distracting her. A nurse wheeled a cart into the hall and disappeared around the corner.

"I can't stand it," she said. "I'm done waiting."

Before she could push into Gwyn's room, a doctor stepped out, stopping Rylie short. "What's wrong?" she asked when he looked up from his chart. She felt breathless, like she had been running, even though she could have run for miles without becoming winded.

"Ms. Gresham is resting," he said, glancing at his cell phone. "She fainted and hit her head, but she's alert now."

"Will she be okay?"

"That's a tough question with a complicated answer."

He checked his phone again. Rylie wanted to grab his shirt and shake him. How could anything be more important than her aunt? Only Seth's steadying hand on her arm—where had he come from?—kept her from doing something stupid.

"Rylie?"

Hearing her aunt's weak voice made every violent thought vanish. Rylie pushed the doctor aside and went inside.

Gwyn had a needle in her arm and a couple bags of fluid hanging over her head. Rylie's heart fragmented into a hundred pieces to see it. She sank into the chair at her side.

"Still not dead, babe," Gwyn said. Her words croaked, so she cleared her throat before speaking again. "Stop looking like you're in mourning."

Rylie had promised herself she wouldn't cry anymore, but seeing her aunt looking so small and helpless in a hospital bed was too much. Her dad's death was frighteningly sudden—one day, he kissed her goodbye, and the next, a counselor was giving her the bad news—and she wasn't sure if it was worse losing a family member quickly or not.

Teardrops plopped on the backs of her hands. She sniffled hard and wiped them on her jeans. "You fell," Rylie said. It was difficult to speak around the lump in her throat.

"Everybody falls."

"Not everybody is sick, though. I knew you were getting worse!"

"I've been feeling fine," she insisted. "But... I haven't watched my t-cell counts as closely as I should, and I didn't like how my medication made me feel. So I didn't take a lot of it." Anger burst in Rylie's chest, but Gwyn touched her hand before she could speak. The IV was taped to her wrist. "Everybody falls. Everybody makes mistakes."

"Mistakes like this could kill you," Rylie said.

"Sometimes the treatment feels worse than the disease. You'll understand someday—hopefully not anytime soon." She sighed. "But you're right. Now we're both paying the price."

Dread settled like a lead weight in Rylie's stomach. "What's happened?"

"What I have is... well, it's kind of like a cold. But it's a terrible cold my body can't fight. My immune system's shot. When I rode Butch out to check on a heifer, it got hard to breathe, and I passed out. No big worry there. But it's caused by a more serious problem." Gwyn's thumb rubbed across the back of Rylie's hand. "I'm going to be in the hospital for a couple days."

"I'll take care of the herd," Rylie said. "I'll move them to the barn myself. I can—"

"You can make them run away, that's what you can do. You're terrible with the cattle. Call Abel. He'll know what needs done."

"Is that why you've had him around so much? Have you been planning to get hospitalized?"

"Nobody *plans* to be sick, babe."

Gwyn sagged against the pillow, like all that talking had exhausted her. It probably had.

Rylie glared at the toe of her boots, stung by the thought that her aunt's preparations for a worst case scenario involved getting Abel to help—Abel, of all people—instead of her niece.

"I'll call him," she said without looking up.

"You'll have to call your mom, too. Jessica needs to know."

Her gaze shot to Gwyn's face. "What?"

"Like it or not, she's still your mother," she said. She couldn't seem to work up the strength to look stern, though she tried.

"But—"

"Seth can come in, you know. Don't make the boy wait outside."

Rylie hadn't realized he was still in the hall. The door was half-open, and she could see the corner of a leather jacket on the other side. He must have been listening to their conversation. He stepped in and grabbed Rylie's hand.

"Ms. Gresham," he said, a little too formally. He cracked a smile. It wasn't his usual bright grin. "You've looked better."

"There's no point trying to impress me now. Make sure Rylie takes care of herself. You got me? And have fun at the Winter Ball. I'll be disappointed if I spent all that money on a beautiful dress and find out you two moped around all night."

"I can't go to the dance now," Rylie said.

Gwyn's hand tightened. "You can and you will. Now go away. You're worrying yourself sick, and that'll make me sicker. I want to see what's happening on General Hospital. I haven't watched it in years." And then she acted like Rylie and Seth no longer existed.

Rylie couldn't feel the floor beneath her feet as she drifted into the hallway. The sights and smells and sounds of the hospital were distant and meaningless.

She didn't realize she was chewing on her thumb again until Seth grabbed her.

"I'll call Abel. Don't eat your hand while I'm gone," he said, pulling out his cell phone and heading outside.

Rylie watched the ripped skin around her nail heal in a daze.

The blood was gone as soon as she wiped it on her jeans, but it planted the seed of an idea that stuck. AIDS was a disease that meant Gwyn couldn't heal. Rylie healed better and faster than any human—she could fix any injury that wasn't inflicted by silver.

What would happen if she turned Gwyn into a werewolf?

Thirteen

Suspicion

Seth stepped out of Rylie's bedroom and shut the door silently behind him. He didn't have to be quiet. She had been asleep the instant he lay her in bed and brushed a kiss on her cheek. She hadn't even gotten out of her sweater.

He sat on the stoop outside. Icicles dripped onto puddles of frost around the porch, and the chair crunched with ice when he sank into it. The cold seeped into his jeans.

Leaning his elbows on his knees, he stared out at the fields, and the dark shape of his brother at work.

Seeing Gwyn in the hospital disturbed him, but not half as much as the news report. He kept rereading the coroner's reports he had copied and thinking of what Rylie said about the murders—that maybe they had trusted their killer.

Abel was herding the cattle into the barn. He used the ATV to do it instead of a horse.

Seth couldn't remember the last time he saw his brother on horseback.

"It can't be," he murmured.

His brother was a lot of things. Brutal, occasionally cruel, intense. But was he a murderer?

Seth saw Rylie's favorite horse wandering outside the fence and went down to catch him. Butch was still saddled. He caught the horse's bridle and guided him to the stables, keeping Abel in the corner of his eye. He rode around the perimeter of the herd, bellowing occasionally to keep them in line.

It was warm inside the stables, and it smelled like hay and manure. Seth removed Butch's tack, hung the saddle on a post, and brushed him down.

"How is she?"

His hand paused mid-brush. Seth glanced over his shoulder to see Abel dismounting the ATV outside the door. The other horses nickered softly.

"She's going to be in the hospital a couple days," Seth said. When Butch huffed and shifted, he resumed brushing. "Sounds like a pretty bad cold."

Abel came inside, shoved the door shut, and pulled off his scarf. Had his scars healed around the edges? He didn't look as mangled as before. "What about Rylie?"

"What about her?"

"You know... how's she taking it?"

Seth set down the brush. Butch ambled into his stall without being prompted, sticking his nose into the trough.

"Why do you care?" he asked, folding his arms.

Abel gave a short laugh. "What—can't I be worried?"

"You don't even like Rylie," Seth said.

It took his brother a heartbeat too long to reply. "Yeah. Right." He grabbed a shovel. "Stalls need to be mucked. Let's get it done."

They worked together in silence, filling a wheelbarrow with horse manure. It would be composted later and used to fertilize the orchard when spring came around, but that didn't make it any more pleasant to handle.

Even though it was freezing outside, shoveling brought Seth to a hard sweat in minutes. He stripped his jacket and threw it on the saddle. Abel followed suit. "Is there something you want to tell me?" Seth asked, keeping his focus on the soiled hay. It was hard not to sound accusing.

"Like what?"

"I don't know. Anything."

Abel leaned on the handle of his shovel. "Did Rylie say something to you?"

Seth shook his head, feeling unsettled. What would Rylie have said to him? And when had his brother started worrying about her instead of wishing she was dead?

"I wonder sometimes…" he began, carefully choosing his words. He swallowed hard and started over. "I haven't heard from Mom since she left. I think she's busy on a hunt—I can't think of any other reason she'd be away so long. You know? She's not the type to let us go without a fight."

"You drove her off, bro," Abel said. "You picked a girl over your responsibility as a hunter. You ever consider she's pissed at you?"

Yeah, he had. More than once. "I think she'll be back."

Abel scraped the last of the manure out of the stall. He moved one arm stiffly. It still didn't have a full range of motion since Rylie attacked him as a werewolf. "Yeah. Probably."

"She's unstoppable," Seth said. "There's nothing she likes better than hunting, maybe including us. That's something you got from her." He leaned the shovel against the wall and wiped his hands on his jeans. "So I wonder… why did you stay?"

"You seriously asking me that?"

The horses shifted in their stalls. Seth nodded. "All this sitting around must be driving you crazy. I mean, we come from a family of hunters—killers. You had to know going with Mom would be more interesting than being here."

Abel folded his arms. They were so thick with muscle that they couldn't lay flat on his chest. "Maybe I like having a job."

"Hunting is your job."

"No. Hunting is *your* job, Mr. Destiny. My job is to stick around until you're eighteen so you don't go into foster care."

Seth gritted his teeth. "It's not my destiny. I hate it when you say that."

"What are you saying, man? You want to get rid of me?"

"I'm just wondering what's going on in your ugly head," Seth said, giving a thin smile. "This stuff, this ranch thing... this isn't normal for you."

Abel studied him. "If you're trying to say something, you better say it."

Are you killing people because you're restless?

Seth shook his head.

"You know what? Forget it." He turned around to grab his jacket and gloves.

He heard the motion before he saw it.

Seth ducked, and Abel's fist smashed into the post above his head. It cracked the wood.

Spinning, he swept out a leg and hooked it behind Abel's ankle. He jerked. Abel stumbled, reaching out both hands for the nearest thing he could find—Seth's shirt.

They toppled together.

Abel used their momentum to roll on top, rearing back to swing a right-hook into Seth's jaw.

The room exploded with black stars. His skull rang.

When he swung again, Seth caught his wrist in a crushing grip, blinking rapidly to clear his vision. He could barely make out Abel's white-toothed grin through the haze.

He snapped forward and head-butted Abel in the nose. His brother bellowed.

Seth shoved him back against the wall, punching him in the gut hard. He aimed for the floating ribs. Abel twisted and made him miss—just barely.

Scurrying to his feet, he tried to back off and get out of his brother's range. But Abel lowered his shoulder and plowed into him like a linebacker, smashing them both into the wall. The entire barn shuddered.

The back of Seth's head bounced on the wall.

Suddenly, he was on the floor looking at the ceiling.

"Ugh," he groaned, grabbing his head. Pain radiated down his spine and shoulders.

Abel offered him a hand. "Dude," he said, still grinning but no longer on the attack, "you blacked out. What a wimp."

"Did you get the license plate on the train that hit me?"

"Don't be such a baby. Get up."

Seth gripped Abel's wrist and let him haul him into a sitting position. He flopped against the wall. "What was that? Are you trying to kill me?"

Abel guffawed as he wiped his mouth on the back of his hand. Blood shone on his knuckles. "Nah. You're a punk. You deserved it, that's all." He looped his arm around his brother's neck and pulled him in for a noogie, but Seth shoved him off. His head hurt way too much for that.

"Yeah, and you're an inbred moron. I better not have any bruises tomorrow. Rylie's going to be mad if I show up for the Winter Ball looking like ground beef."

"If I'm inbred, you know what that says about you," Abel said. "Explains your stupid face, doesn't it?"

Seth couldn't help it. He laughed. But the image of Isaiah Branson crept into his mind, like inky tendrils of fear, and his laughter died.

"Winter Ball, huh?" Abel mused that with a sour look. "Sounds pretty gay."

"You're pretty gay," Seth muttered. Not his best comeback, but his head still felt like a shattered bell.

"Nice. Real nice."

They sat together on the floor, backs against the wall, and listened to the wind rising outside. Cold seeped through a crack in the window. After a few minutes, Seth didn't feel quite so terrible, and his eyes could actually focus again. He squinted at his brother.

The first time Abel had been bitten by a werewolf had thrown them into a hellish three-month nightmare. The battle against the curse was the hardest they fought in their life until Seth met Rylie.

As much as they fought, they were more than brothers. They were best friends.

Or at least, they used to be.

"You can tell me whatever. You know that, right?" Seth asked. Abel's smile faded. He nodded.

Seth's first attempt to stand failed, so Abel helped him up. He started grinning again. "Your eye looks awesome," he said. "That's going to be a nice shiner."

"You jerk," Seth said, giving him a small shove.

"You're welcome."

Abel didn't put his coat on again before mounting the ATV to take it to the shed. Seth followed him more slowly on foot.

His brother couldn't have killed anyone. He was scary sometimes, but he wasn't crazy—and there was compassion in there somewhere deep down. *Really* deep down.

It had to be someone else killing. Seth was sure of it.

Mostly.

• ◯ •

Christmas Eve arrived, and so did the day of the Winter Ball. Rylie woke up as exhausted that morning as she had every other morning for weeks and found she didn't have the energy to get out of bed.

Her dress—that gorgeous dress—hung over her door where she could see it. But she couldn't move. Her thoughts overwhelmed her.

Gwyn was still in the hospital and might not come back.

She could only learn to control the change if she left Seth.

There were hunters outside her home with guns—right now—searching for things to shoot at, and they wouldn't care if they spotted coyotes or wolves.

And she was going to change into a monster again that very night, whether she liked it or not.

It was all too much. Hugging her pillow to her chest and hiking the sheets to her shoulders, Rylie burrowed into her bed and wished it would turn into a big stone sarcophagus to entomb her away from life.

She heard engine sounds through her shut window and detected a faint smell that meant Abel was nearby. He would take care of the ranch. At least that was one less thing to worry about. It was strange to feel grateful for his presence.

But she smelled Seth too, and didn't want to face him. She originally planned to dress up and surprise him, but she couldn't imagine getting in the shower anymore, much less doing her hair and makeup.

Someone knocked on her door. She didn't move.

"Are you awake?"

Seth didn't raise his voice, like he was trying not to wake her up. She stayed silent so he would think she was sleeping.

Even though she didn't move, the door opened and he slipped in. He sat on the edge of her bed. "I can't do this," Rylie mumbled. "Any of it."

Seth kicked off his shoes. She lifted the covers and he climbed underneath them, spooning his body around hers. His arm was warm and secure and safe around her stomach.

"Yeah. It sucks."

They stayed there all morning.

Eventually, Rylie got too hungry to stay in bed. Seth left to get his tuxedo, and she took a plate of barely-cooked bacon into her room for breakfast. She stared at her dress as she chewed on it.

How was she supposed to put that giant thing on without Gwyn's help?

She washed her hands off before wrestling it over her head, twisting her arms around to zip it halfway up her back. Rylie studied herself in the full-length mirror on her wardrobe door, heavy with helplessness.

It was a full-length ball gown with layers of blue silk. Against her winter-pale skin and white blonde hair, she looked like an ice fairy. The high waist made her legs impossibly long. It sparkled with tiny beads. Even without her makeup done, she looked amazing.

She closed the wardrobe so she wouldn't have to see herself anymore.

Rylie did her hair in a loose bun and added sparkly clips to match her flowing skirt. Even though she kept her makeup simple, by the time she finished, she heard Seth come in the front door. She stepped out of the bathroom to find him waiting in the living room.

Seth's mouth dropped open, and all the hours she spent wrestling with herself over the dress and the dance were instantly worth it. He looked amazing in a tuxedo. It made him look taller, broader, and all around manlier. The ice blue tie with his black shirt and jacket matched Rylie's dress perfectly.

And he only had eyes for her.

How long had she been holding her breath? She felt lightheaded.

Somehow she drifted toward him, closing the gap between their bodies, but she didn't remember taking a single step. "You're beautiful," Seth said.

She bit her bottom lip. That was basically her thoughts about him, too, except punctuated by "hot" and "oh my God" and incoherent babbling noises.

"You're late," she teased, trying to bring her brain back to Earth before she lost herself in Seth's crooked smile. Rylie stretched up to kiss him, but he pulled back and cleared his throat. "What...?"

"Cute. Really cute."

Abel stood in the doorway, dirty and sweat-soaked despite the snow outside. She dropped back on her heels and rolled her eyes. "Great, just who I wanted to see."

He arched an eyebrow at her. "Nice dress."

"What are you doing tonight while we're out?" Seth asked, stepping forward to shield Rylie from him.

"I have plans," Abel said airily. "Don't worry about me. Have fun, children." He was only nineteen. She fought not to roll her eyes again. She didn't want them to fall out of her head.

She wrapped herself in a fake fur shrug and held hands with Seth as they walked out to the truck. He waited until they both climbed in to pull a box out of his jacket.

Rylie gasped. There was a gorgeous white flower in full bloom inside, glittering with dew.

"I got this for you," he said. "But I don't want you to feel like you have to go to this, no matter what Gwyneth said. We can stay home if you want. Your night's going to be hard enough after the moon rises."

She took a deep breath. "I want to go. I do." She couldn't muster very much conviction.

Rylie held out her arm. He put the corsage on her wrist, fingers lingering on her skin. "We'll do this together," Seth said. "You don't have to be alone."

For the first time that day, she smiled.

"Thank you."

Fourteen

The Winter Ball

Seth and Rylie arrived at the dance late and had to park all the way on the top floor of the parking garage (which only had two levels). He put on a watch before getting out of the truck. "It's after six now," he said. "The moon shouldn't hit until eleven, but we'll need to leave by nine to get home in time. Tell me when you feel the wolf."

Rylie nodded. He offered his arm, and they walked out together. The stairs were decorated with balloons, and the sidewalk toward the hall was draped in fluttering ribbons. It was like standing in a storm of silk.

The line to get in stretched all the way to the road, so they took position at the back. She craned around to see through the doorway. Everything inside was decorated in twinkling lights and glitter, and the room shimmered as though encrusted in snow. An ice sculpture of a swan guarded the entrance.

She gasped, holding tight to Seth's arm. "Do you see that?"

"It's beautiful," he said. He wasn't looking at the decorations.

She hoped it was too dark for him to see her blushing.

Seth kissed her, but they couldn't enjoy the moment for long. It was too cold. A crowd of high school students came in from the parking garage and caught them in their hurry to get indoors. They were swept inside.

The building was already packed. Rylie had no idea there were so many teenagers in the whole state. The leadership committees had done an awesome job: there was a whole table of food against the wall, including giant strawberries dipped in chocolate, and (even better) platters of meat and cheese.

Smells surrounded Rylie, crashing into each other until they were impossible to distinguish. Perfumes. Lotions. Sweat. Shampoo. Food. The fake mist coming out of the machines on the dance floor. Cigarette smoke. Even the ice by the doorway.

And, of course, other wolves.

Her eye fell on a girl in a white dress at the other end of the room. Bekah smiled and wiggled her fingers in a little wave. After her talk with Scott Whyte, she wasn't sure how to respond.

After a moment, Rylie waved back.

Seth nudged her. "Do you see that?"

People were clustered around the door. Through a gap in the bodies, Rylie saw Tate in a white tuxedo with Levi on his arm. Tate was making a huge scene, of course. He was all about the attention, and there wasn't anything more attention-grabbing than the son of the county commissioner showing up with his boyfriend.

Rylie had to laugh. Tate always knew exactly what would piss off his parents.

"This is going to end up in the newspaper. I bet you anything," she said. "In fact, I'd be surprised if Tate doesn't submit it himself."

"Tate's gay?"

"I'm way more worried that he's dating *Levi*. Aren't you?"

"But... they're both guys."

She stared at him, trying to decide if he was serious or not. Maybe he was. Rylie was from a big city, where plenty of kids had been openly gay, or had been raised in families with same-sex parents. But Seth had been raised isolated from the rest of the world. The only people he knew were the ones he hunted.

"You know Gwyn likes other women, right?" Rylie asked.

"*What*?"

"Sure. When I was little, she lived with a woman named Jane," she said. Seth looked so shocked that she almost felt bad for him. She laughed and pushed him gently. "Whatever, Mr. I Kill Werewolves for Fun. Glass houses and stones and stuff."

His mouth opened and shut soundlessly. "But—"

Tate's attention storm blew past them. He stopped long enough to give Rylie a big hug—which nearly gagged her with the smell of pot smoke—and then dragged his date onto the dance floor. Levi seemed almost as stunned as everyone else. That was life in the Tate Zone.

When he was gone again, Seth looked nauseated. Rylie decided to ignore him.

She tugged on his hand. "Dance with me."

The floor was packed. Kids in formal dresses bounced around to club music, which would have been funny to see if it hadn't been so dark. It made everything intimate, even though the room was full.

Closer to the speakers, the music blasted through her bones and made her blood shake. There was a time Rylie loved going to concerts. Having a DJ put on the music wasn't the same thing as a live band, but it was almost as good.

The bass thump-thumped in her chest and drowned everything else out—even her worries, for a few minutes.

Neither Seth nor Rylie were good dancers. He wasn't coordinated, and she didn't have a sense of rhythm. But they were bad dancers together. When Seth twirled her for the third time, she had to start laughing. She almost forgot to be upset about everything.

Until she spotted Scott Whyte standing among the chaperones in the back.

She tripped on her own dress. Seth caught her, and she stiffened at his touch.

The wolf came roaring to the surface.

The smells.

Everything she had been trying to ignore crashed down on her. The smells, the sounds, the sensation of bodies crowded around her. It was suddenly all too much. Her skin flushed with a wave of heat.

Her fingernails dug into Seth's arms. "What's wrong?" he shouted. She could barely hear him over the music.

She shook her head. How could she tell him that the werewolf was rising early? There was too much sensory input. Too many smells.

He spotted Bekah and recognition dawned.

"Let's take a break," Seth said.

The back hallway was empty aside from a couple looking for a sneaky place to make out. Rylie ducked into an alcove and braced her back against the wall, pressing her hands against her forehead.

Hungry.

"Shut up. You're *always* hungry," she whispered to the wolf.

Seth squeezed her hand. "I'll be right back."

When he came back, he had a paper plate stacked with thin-sliced sausage and ham. He held it for Rylie while she scarfed it down. Satiating one hunger made it easier to control the wolf, but only a little.

"That witch is here," she said between bites.

"I don't think they want to hurt you."

She shook her head. No, they weren't there to hurt her. They wanted to take her away. But why now? Why couldn't they let her have a night to herself? "I need to sit down."

They found an unoccupied bench and took it. The music was distant and muffled from the end of the hall. Cold air leeched through the doors. Rylie's skin was burning, so she barely felt it.

The moon was outside. She couldn't see it, but she knew it was there. She always knew where the moon was located, like a fragment of her soul suspended in space. Being close to the exit didn't help. Her fingernails itched.

She spread her fingers in front of her and saw the first dots of blood appear around the edges.

"Are you going to change? Should we—?"

"I'm fine. Give me a second."

She ducked into the bathroom. Girls she didn't recognize were fixing their makeup in the mirror and leaning forward to adjust their cleavage. There was a line waiting for a stall, but Rylie took the first open toilet.

"Hey!" someone protested.

Without bothering to apologize, she locked the door and yanked a fistful of toilet paper off the roll. She pressed it to her fingers.

I'm not going to change. I'm human. I'm not going to change.

She closed her eyes, took deep breaths, and focused on relaxing her muscles one at a time.

Slowly, her nerves settled. Her hands stopped shaking. Her skin cooled. She pushed back the supernaturally strong scents of the bathroom until she could pretend she had a normal sense of smell. And then she washed her hands—fingernails intact—and returned to Seth.

He smiled that knee-weakening smile when he saw her.

"You okay?" he asked. "You want to dance?"

She nodded.

They avoided the corner where Scott Whyte had been lurking on their way back in. Seth pulled her onto the dance floor. Rylie shut her eyes and moved to the beat without thinking about it.

His arms enveloped her. They moved together, from right foot to left foot and back again, without paying attention to the world around them. Nothing else mattered. It was just them— two normal humans having fun.

That was all.

•○•

The night was a blur of dancing and food. Bekah and Scott stayed out of the way. Tate drew a crowd with his inappropriate dancing and loud singing, which made Rylie laugh and clap from the sidelines. She ate a lot of hors d'oeuvres, danced with Seth for what felt like hours, and tried to forget she would be changing soon.

But the wolf wouldn't let her forget.

The moon crept in on her. Eventually, she couldn't ignore it anymore. It was nine o'clock. "We should leave," she said.

Seth grinned. "One more dance."

They took the dance floor, and Rylie leaned against him with her eyes closed. They slow-danced to fast music. When she opened her eyes, Seth was staring straight down at her.

Rylie pushed herself onto her toes to kiss him. There was nothing in the world but them, and their bodies, and the absence of space between them. His hands on her back were the only thing holding her inside her skin. Her *human* skin.

When she pulled back, his eyes glowed as they raked down her body. She wasn't the only hungry one.

But then something caught his attention, and Seth's eyes focused over her head. His face fell. "Oh no. Oh, this is bad, this is really bad—"

Rylie didn't need to follow his gaze to the door to smell who had just entered. His scent gusted toward her as he sauntered into the room.

Abel.

She had to admit he looked good in a button-up shirt and slacks, scarred face and all. His muscular arms and chest were accentuated by the sharp lines of the shirt. He looked like Seth, if he was run through a meat grinder and came out meaner on the other side.

The corner of Abel's mouth lifted in a smirk when he saw them, but he didn't approach. He ambled toward the snack table and started picking out pieces of salami.

There were enough students from the different schools that nobody would notice if someone showed up uninvited, but Abel didn't look like a student. He was young, but not *that* young— and the scars were too distinctive.

"What should we do?" Rylie asked.

Tension made hard lines stand out in Seth's throat. "I should talk to him. He can't be here for anything good."

"He'll get kicked out, right?" she whispered.

He responded by pulling Rylie deeper onto the dance floor, where other bodies buffeted against theirs and hid them from the periphery of the room. Her nerves were ringing.

The hard dance beat died, and the DJ put on a slow song. Students started moving off the floor. They were exposed.

"Let's just go," she said.

But it was too late. Abel strode up to them, effortlessly parting the crowd, and focused on Rylie like Seth wasn't even there. "Dance with me," he said. It wasn't a question.

Revulsion shocked through Rylie. Seth stepped forward. "What the heck, man? No way."

"Let her answer for herself."

Her first impulse involved a lot of swear words, but there was something imploring in his dark eyes. Her wolf was happy to see him, even if the rest of her wasn't so enthusiastic.

"Fine," she said.

Seth's mouth fell open. "Rylie, you don't have to—"

"I know."

"Great. Make yourself disappear, kid," Abel said, giving his brother a light shove. He took Rylie's hand and led her to the middle of the dance floor. The students gave them plenty of space. Given Abel's size, they had no other choice.

Seth took a seat in the corner, looking furious.

She settled her free hand lightly on his upper arm and met his eyes defiantly. "What are you trying to do?" she asked.

"Maybe I want to have fun."

"I can't imagine you crashing a high school dance for fun."

Abel turned suddenly serious. "All right. Seth asked me why I stayed when I should have left with our mom. And I thought—well, Gwyn drew up paperwork to give me the ranch. It's in her will. If she dies, the ranch gets turned over to me and Seth. Mostly me."

Rylie had been prepared for a lot of things to come out of his mouth, but that wasn't one of them. She stopped moving. "What?" The ache that had grown lighter during the dance came crashing back on her like a huge fist between her ribs. She could barely breathe. "Why would she do that? She's not going to die, is she?"

"She's ready for it."

Rylie covered her mouth with a hand. "Oh my God."

There was sadness on Abel's face, actual sadness. "She's been nice to me. Nobody's ever been that nice to me. She treats me like a person—not some dumb piece of trash." His Adam's apple bobbed when he swallowed hard. "You and me might be family someday, but Gwyn's already better than my real family, except my dork of a brother. So I guess you and me are pack." Abel shook his head and quickly changed it to, "Family. Not pack."

But he was right. The first word resonated with her much more than the second.

"You're pack," Rylie said, testing the words on her tongue.

They weren't pretending to dance at all anymore. Abel's hands squeezed tight on her waist. It hurt enough to stir the wolf again.

Stiffly, he nodded.

She couldn't see Seth anymore. The crowd was too thick and the room was dark, isolating them from the rest of the world. One of the lights by the DJ booth spun, bathing them in light for a short second. His eyes flashed with gold.

"When did that happen?' she asked.

"When you bit me," he said. "After that... I started changing again. Like the first time I was attacked, but different."

"Are you becoming a werewolf?"

"I don't know. I can't remember." Pain flashed across his face. "*I can't remember.*"

Rylie knew his pain, because she felt it too. She had never remembered what happened on the full and new moons, but she had begun forgetting all her other nights, too. It scared her in a way nothing else had scared her before.

"It will be okay. We're pack," she said forcefully.

Impulsively, she reached up and touched his scarred cheek. The skin was softer than it looked. Rylie traced a line from his temple to his jaw. It looked like the skin had been ripped off his head and grown back the wrong way.

A whole chunk in the shell of his ear was missing. A pink gouge marked his jaw.

His eyes shut tight.

"We're pack," Rylie said again, softer this time. "I'll take care of you." She dropped her hand. "Thanks. You know, for telling me about Gwyn. Is that why you came here?"

"No." A hint of his old, dangerous smile returned. "I came here to kill those wolf kids."

She stiffened. "*What?*"

"Quiet," he said when people turned to look at them. The song was almost over and they were out of time. Abel stepped in close. He was holding that big knife again even though she hadn't seen him draw it. He hid it between their bodies. "You know it's got to be done."

"But—I don't think—"

The smell of silver was too distracting. She choked on sudden rage. He went on before she could speak. "You're changing tonight. Maybe I am, too. Who cares? Let's do it. We'll end it. Both of them at the same time."

"With all these people here?" she growled.

Scott Whyte appeared out of the crowd and tapped Abel on the shoulder. "I don't think you have an invitation."

Abel pressed himself against Rylie, wrapping his arm around her back in an iron grip. She felt the hard press of the knife against her stomach as he tried to hide it.

"You got a problem?" he spat.

Scott held up his hands in the universal gesture of peace. There was no way he could out-intimidate Abel. He was shorter, heavier, and forty years too old. "This isn't the place. Why don't we talk outside?"

Abel's lip peeled back. "Don't think I won't take care of you too."

They were attracting attention. People had stopped dancing and turned to watch them, stepping back to make space on the dance floor. Rylie's cheeks flamed.

"Abel," she whispered, tugging on his arm. The music picked up again, and she spoke quietly enough that Scott wouldn't be able to hear her. "We can't do this here. People will get hurt."

His eyes flicked between Rylie and Scott. She felt him falter. "Outside," said the older man.

Abel stepped back with a sharp nod.

She hadn't seen him approach, but Seth was hovering nearby, waiting to intervene.

"Follow them," she mouthed.

All three men went outside. Levi broke away from Tate at the back of the room and followed.

Rylie sat heavily at a table. Her body was wracked with shivers. She hadn't realized how strongly the confrontation affected her until she realized her gums were aching and her fingernails were bleeding again.

The moon called to her. Rylie couldn't push it away.

And then Bekah Riese sat at her table.

"We don't have much time," Bekah said. "My dad will try to distract them for as long as he can, but—well, you need to come with me. And fast."

"Back off," Rylie said.

It wasn't a threat. It was a warning. Her heart was pounding, driving blood like molten lava through her veins.

"Me and Levi haven't hurt anyone, and I don't have to tell you it isn't coyotes. Right?" she whispered. "But if it's not us, and it's not you, then that leaves a big question jumping out at us, doesn't it?"

"Who would it be?"

"Exactly."

The full force of Bekah's suggestion struck her.

Could Abel be the killer?

"No," she said. "No way. Why should I believe you? You've moved in on my territory, and you—"

"We're here to save you. There's only ever been one person bent on turning this into a territory battle. Think about it. You know it's true."

Bekah tried to pull Rylie away from the table. She shook her off. "Don't touch me!"

"I wanted to tell you sooner, but him and his brother are always around you. Please, Rylie, they're dangerous. You have to come with me."

"I'm not safe tonight." Her voice came out rough, like it did shortly before the change.

"We have a safe place for moons. All three of us—you, me, and Levi. Dad told you his specialty is teen wolves, didn't he? But we have to hurry. You're going to change soon. You should see your eyes."

"It's too soon," she whispered.

"You're not in control. Come with me! Please!"

Her muscles shivered under her skin. *So many people...*

The room was crowded with bodies. Hormones ran high. They were all on edge, and all so tender.

Nobody would expect an attack. She could feast.

Seth's hands caught her shoulders from behind. The comfort of his skin brought her human mind back to the surface, if only a little bit. She stepped back into his arms and leaned against him.

"Back off," he barked at Bekah, and her eyes went wide and round. "You heard me! Go!"

"Rylie…"

He dragged her toward the doors. Abel was waiting outside.

"We have to hurry," Seth said. "You're changing."

Fifteen

Cold and Dark

Rylie felt drawn to get in the Chevelle with Abel, but Seth threw her into the truck. "Not now," he said sharply.

"Bekah said Abel's killing people," she said.

Seth put the truck into gear and roared out of the parking garage. "That's what Scott said, too."

"It's not possible. Is it?"

His eyes cut over to her. "Rylie…" His knuckles were white on the steering wheel. "I've had suspicions, but there's an easy way to find out. We'll lock both of you up. If people die tonight, we'll know it couldn't have been him."

"And if nobody dies?"

He didn't respond.

Seth had prepared a safe place for Rylie to change after hunters began combing the wilderness for coyotes. It was an old cellar beneath an unoccupied farmhouse a couple miles from the ranch, and they had to race to make it there in time.

Rylie hadn't expected he would lock Abel up in there on the moon, too.

She had to keep her forehead pressed to her knees to keep from getting sick as they drove. Seeing the night sky was too much. It made the wolf want to run into the darkness searching for prey.

The Chevelle beat them to the cellar. Abel leaned against the hood, arms folded tight and brow drawn low over his eyes.

"Let's get this over with," he said.

Seth stopped him before he could go inside. "Let Rylie get ready first."

Get ready? She looked down at her dress and realized she would have to strip if she didn't want to destroy it. She hadn't been able to figure out a way to change with her clothes on. The build of the wolf was too weird—aside from being four-legged and hairy, she developed a lot of chest muscle that she didn't have as a human, and her body became as thick around as a keg of beer.

And the tail was another thing entirely.

"Can we change in different places?" Rylie whispered, clinging to Seth's arm. She tried to keep her skirt out of the snow, but the hem was already soggy. "Please?"

He rubbed her shoulders. "I don't know anywhere else secure to put him, and we're out of time. This is all we have."

"But what if Abel isn't becoming a werewolf again? What if he's still human, and I hurt him?"

"You'll both be tied up tight. Don't worry."

Rylie went into the cellar alone. The air was musty and stale. Cobwebs clung to the low ceiling. Dusty old boxes were labeled with things like "Vacation 1983" and "Christmas decorations," but it looked like Seth had cleared a dark, empty corner for her.

She stripped to her underwear. Knowing she would have to transform after the dance, she had spent way too long trying to decide if she should wear something sexy or modest—though she had only expected Seth to see it. She picked a strapless bra and panties with lacy parts on the sides. Now she wished she had worn long johns.

Seth joined her after a minute and laid a blanket around her shoulders. "I'm not cold," she said.

"Keep it anyway." He was bundled up in a leather jacket, gloves, and a scarf over his tuxedo, and he still looked like he was freezing.

The stairs creaked as Abel came down. He looked even bigger without a shirt on. The scars on his face went all the way down his chest and side, breaking up the black curls that covered his torso.

Seth dropped black ropes and thick steel chains on the ground. Rylie shuddered. She remembered those way too well.

He separated out some of the ropes and tossed them to Abel before sitting next to her. Seth touched her cheek. "You okay? You're being awfully quiet."

She tried to smile and failed. "I don't want to do this."

"I know. I'm sorry."

Seth helped Abel with the restraints first. As soon as his wrists were bound, she pulled the loose rigging over her head. It sagged in the front where her muzzle would grow to fill it. She did the latch in the back with shaking fingers, then fit her hands into the wrist loops and wrapped the ropes around her ankles.

Seth had to tighten the chains for her. They pinched.

"Comfortable?" he asked.

"Not really. You've upgraded." She pillowed her head on her arms while he cinched the ankles tight.

"You used to be weaker."

Seth checked the ropes one last time, gave her a kiss, and tossed her voluminous dress over his shoulder. "Where are you going?" she asked.

"I'll be right outside. Just think… when you guys wake up, it will be Christmas Eve."

"Yeah. Merry freaking Christmas," Abel muttered. He sat stiffly in the corner with his chains looped around a wall hook.

"Lay out my dress so it doesn't get wrinkled," she said.

Seth winked at her. It was probably meant to be encouraging.

Once he shut the doors and latched the lock, it was quiet in the cellar. Rylie stretched out as much as she could and tried to get comfortable, but something about being hogtied made relaxing impossible.

"Are you scared?" Rylie asked.

Abel folded his arms on his knees and didn't respond. He definitely smelled scared.

A familiar shudder rolled through her body. She gasped.

It was time.

Her fingernails had already fallen out, and her jaw had begun to shift, so she felt it in her spine first this time. Her lower back snapped and began to grind, like two rocks smashing her spinal column.

She thought it would hurt less if she changed more often. But it didn't. It only got worse.

Her tailbone erupted from her back and wrenched free with a sick *pop*. Her chin cracked and spread forward as her ears slid up the sides of her head.

Rylie screamed—she always screamed—and she registered the smell of adrenaline coming off Abel.

Her chains rattled as she writhed. Her shoulders twisted as she strained to break free. Heat spread down her neck, shoulders, and hips as fur emerged. Her bra snapped off as her breastbone spread.

She swelled within her bindings. The ropes pulled tight against her wrists. Her face filled the muzzle.

As her body expanded within the ropes, the wolf expanded within her mind. It took control. Calm settled over her. A sense of peace—until it realized it was bound.

The wolf thrashed, growling and snapping and straining to chew at the chains. But the muzzle held its mouth shut, and that only made it angrier.

Abel's screams pierced through her frenzy. She tried to get to her feet to help him, but she couldn't.

His human body distorted as the wolf fought to come through. His skin bulged in strange places. His back arched and his feet drummed against the floor.

And then he became a wolf.

Seth got in the truck, turned on the heater, and prepared to spend the night staked out by the cellar.

He thought he could get some studying done. He wanted to make up time he had lost to recent distractions, so he had brought everything with him even though they were on winter break for the next two weeks: binders, text books, note cards, the works.

"Muscle memory," he read aloud off his notes. It was cold enough in the truck that his breath fogged.

Cerebellum. Easy stuff.

He imagined Rylie sitting next to him, cheeks pink with cold and a big smile on her face. Teasing him for cheating even though he hadn't. Promising to let him operate on her brain. They both knew his chances of getting into medical school weren't great, but she would have supported him through anything.

She was in the cellar—right now—in immense agony.

Trapped with his brother.

Seth dropped the cards and stared out the window at the snowy night. He hadn't been shocked when Scott Whyte took him outside the dance to tell him that Abel was a werewolf. He wasn't even shocked when the psychologist accused him of being the murderer and said they should leave town.

What surprised him was how jealous he became when Abel demanded to dance with Rylie.

Those powerful, possessive feelings had come from nowhere. He didn't like the thought of Rylie giving Abel that dimpled smile.

What kind of game was he playing? Asking his brother's girlfriend to *dance*?

He made himself pick up the flash cards again.

Heartbeat. That was the brainstem.

Which part of the brain controlled jealousy?

He threw the cards across the dashboard. No way would he get any studying done with thoughts like those.

Motion on the horizon caught his eye. For a moment, Seth thought it was the wind blowing through the trees, but then a light flickered. It wasn't a star—it was a flashlight.

The hunters, he realized. Rangers and cops looking for coyotes to shoot.

He glanced at the cellar door. It was locked from the outside.

The hunters didn't turn in his direction. The silhouettes on the horizon stayed on the horizon, then faded as they went the other way. The tension in his shoulders relaxed. It would be a long night.

Seth stretched out on the bench seat and pulled his jacket around his face. A tangled mess of emotions knotted in his chest. The fear that his brother might have lost his fight to stay human was the worst, but the jealousy was a close second.

He didn't mean to sleep. He wanted to wait until the hunters were gone, and then check to see if Abel had changed.

But his eyes were so heavy. He relaxed into the seat.

The truck warmed with his body heat. Engine sounds made him drift. It was a little like Rylie's angry growl, which he thought was kind of cute—not that he ever would have told her that.

He hoped she was okay in the cellar...

A bang made him startle.

Seth sat upright. His body was slow. A glance at the dash clock told him he had fallen asleep—and worse, he had slept through most of the night. It was already four in the morning.

A second bang reminded him why he woke up. He rubbed his hand over the foggy window to see the cellar door shudder.

The door burst open, and a dark shape exploded from the depths of the cellar.

No—two shapes.

Seth's stomach pitched. He seized his rifle, leaped out of the truck, and almost slipped in the snow. A few extra inches had accumulated in the hours he was unconscious.

"Wait! Stop!"

One was clearly Rylie. He had seen her golden fur and sleek body enough times to recognize her.

The second figure was unfamiliar. It was a huge, black-furred wolf bigger than a horse. He knew who it had to be. There had only been two people locked in the cellar.

"Abel!"

They chased each other into the darkness.

Seth couldn't run fast enough to keep up with a werewolf, and the truck couldn't go the kind of places they could. He couldn't catch them. He had to outsmart them.

Where would a pair of werewolves go?

No—wait. He wasn't dealing with two of them. There were four. And they wouldn't be able to resist the urge to fight.

He shouldered his rifle and jumped back in the truck. He drove at an angle to Rylie and Abel's path, heart pounding out a bass rhythm in his chest.

Seth took shortcuts through the hills. He didn't see any killer coyotes, hunters, or werewolves by the time he came upon the first houses. He went straight for the Riese house at top speed and jumped out on the driveway. He didn't care if anyone saw him with his gun. There was no time to be discreet.

The entire neighborhood was dark. He prayed nobody would be home.

He didn't feel the itching in the back of his neck that would mean Bekah and Levi were nearby. But the house smelled of them. He was sure they would go there first.

Tires whispered at the end of the street. A white luxury sedan sliced through the snow and stopped in front of the

Riese house. Scott Whyte stepped out into the cold morning with a frown.

"What are you doing here, Seth?" he asked, elbows resting on the open door.

"Get back in the car," he said. "Turn around and go back wherever you came from."

The psychologist sized up the situation—Seth covered in snow with a gun over his shoulder—and seemed to realize what was happening. "They escaped, didn't they?"

"You know where they'll hunt first," Seth said. Scott took a heavy jacket and earmuffs out of the car before slamming the door shut. "What are you doing?"

"I'm going to help you find them."

"What about Bekah and Levi?"

"They're in a safe house," Scott said. "We need to—"

A distant thunderclap echoed over the silent night. Seth's head whipped around. Dark shapes with flashlights—more hunters—ran through the snow in the fields beyond the house.

One of them had fired a gun.

He broke into a run. Scott followed him, huffing and puffing as he fought to keep up.

"Hey!" he yelled when he drew close.

There were two people near the trees: a man in a plaid jacket and a sheriff's deputy. Both of them had their guns drawn. Even in the darkness, Seth could see they were pale.

"Who are you?" asked the deputy.

"He's with me," Scott panted, coming up behind Seth. He leaned on his knees and wheezed. "What happened?"

The deputy seemed to recognize him. Her eyes flicked to Seth's rifle, then back to Scott. Guns were common enough in the country that she didn't seem surprised by it. "You need to get inside, sir."

"Coyotes?" Scott asked.

The hunter in plaid and the deputy exchanged looks. They didn't have to say anything. Their expressions spoke volumes.

They hadn't been shooting coyotes.

"It's not safe out here," said the deputy. "Get in your house and stay there, Mr. Whyte. We're going to follow the trail."

Trail?

Seth realized there was blood in the snow. The world spun around him. Did that belong to Abel, Rylie, or both? Either way, someone had been shot, and not with silver bullets. That was almost worse.

Now there weren't just two werewolves on the loose. There were two *angry* werewolves.

"Thank you," Scott said. "We'll do just that."

The hunters moved for the line of trees, following the dribbles of blood. They had already forgotten about Seth and Scott in their pursuit. The deputy barked into the walkie-talkie on her shoulder.

Seth's scalp tingled. They were close.

"I'll get the restraints," Scott muttered as soon as they were out of earshot.

Seth nodded. He could feel a werewolf to the north, not far from the direction the hunters were headed.

He looped around the trees to avoid the deputy, fingers freezing where they gripped his rifle. The darkness of morning grew lighter. The air turned deep violet as snow showered around him. It was thick and fluffy by the trees.

Soon Seth was up to his knees and breathing hard. It was like running through quicksand. But adrenaline pushed him on.

Gunfire cracked a few feet away, making his ears ring.

In the trees.

Seth dove behind a snow drift and braced his rifle on a boulder, aiming it at a dark form.

The plaid-jacketed hunter was on the ground, his shotgun a few inches from his fingers. His head was bloody where it had hit a rock. The deputy was nowhere in sight.

And a huge black wolf crouched over his body.

Abel looked up. The ruff of fur at his neck was matted with snow, and his gold eyes glinted when he turned them on Seth. There was no mistaking his brother—even as a wolf.

"Oh man," Seth groaned.

His finger trembled on the trigger.

Shoot him, whispered his mother's voice in the back of his head.

Scott crashed through the trees behind him. "Blessed goddess," he breathed when he saw Abel. There were thick black ropes in his arms with locks shaped like silver pentacles.

The sound of his approach started Abel into motion. He lunged.

Seth reacted on instinct. Jumping up, he swung the butt of the rifle with all his strength.

It connected with Abel's face.

He crumpled.

Seth stood over his brother, shoulders heaving as he sucked in huge breaths of cold air. It burned his throat and lungs. His eyes were stinging.

Seth flung the rifle to the ground. He couldn't shoot. He wouldn't.

Even if his brother was a murderer.

"Don't just stand there," Scott said, dropping beside Abel. He expertly wound the ropes around his body and locked them with the silver pentacles, taking care to keep the metal from touching his flesh directly.

Seth edged around him to inspect the body of the hunter, feeling numb inside and out. It looked like Abel had bitten a chunk out of his upper arm, but that wasn't what killed him— that was the head injury.

"Did Abel get shot?" Seth asked.

Scott lifted a bloody hand. There was a bullet between two fingers. "Yes. In the leg."

So Rylie wasn't nearby. He couldn't find it in himself to be glad about that. The grief of finding his brother as a werewolf—a beast that had been killing people—was too powerful.

He sank to his brother's side.

"You screwed up, man," he whispered.

He had to have known he was changing. Why hadn't he asked for help? Maybe Seth couldn't have fixed him, but he could have kept him from killing people.

But now there were eight dead bodies. Abel had ruined his life—both of their lives.

Scott clapped a hand on Seth's back. "You know what you have to do."

Unfortunately, he did.

Sixteen

Christmas

Rylie awoke naked on her own doorstep.

She sat up, brushing snow off her shoulders. The ranch was silent in the early morning hours. All the animals were in the barn or their pens, the fields were empty, and there wasn't a car in sight.

Where was Seth?

She stood on trembling legs and took a sniff of the air. There was no hint of the perfume she sprayed on her clothing, so she couldn't have changed nearby.

Shutting her eyes, she wracked her brain for answers. There had been a dance, hadn't there? She danced with Seth—and Abel, she recalled with some embarrassment—and spoke to Bekah. But everything was a blur after that. She had no idea when or where she changed.

So why was she at home?

She went inside. The floor was so warm on her icy feet that it burned. She held the phone between her ear and shoulder as she called Seth, trying to rub circulation into her extremities.

He didn't pick up. "This is Seth. Leave me a message."

"Call me back," she said, blowing on her fingers. "Or even better, come here. I don't have my truck. What happened?

Where are you?" She hesitated. She wasn't sure if they were at that place in their relationship where she could say she loved him at the end of messages yet. "So... yeah. Bye."

She hung up.

After that, she didn't know what else to do but shower, dress, and do her chores.

But Seth never called her back.

Christmas in the hospital was a muted event. Holiday lights presented a fire hazard and weren't allowed in the ward, but Rylie had brought some dusty old garland from home to hang around Gwyn's bed. She put a couple stuffed Santas and nutcrackers on the windowsill, too. By the time she finished decorating, the room almost looked cheery.

The floor was quiet other than the occasional visit from a nurse. Nobody bothered Rylie as she made a second trip to her truck to retrieve presents, although a few people did stop to open doors for her.

She dropped the presents and stockings at the foot of Gwyn's bed. "Looks great, babe," she said with a weak smile. She was propped up with a saline drip and very pale. "You should be spending Christmas with the boys, though."

Rylie bit her bottom lip. Seth still hadn't called her. The only sign he was still around was that her truck had reappeared at the ranch the night before—but he didn't come in to say hi. "They aren't much for the holidays."

Gwyn touched her hand. "Why so sad?"

"I'm not sad. Here, look in your stocking." She passed it to her aunt and took her own, which Gwyn had filled before her collapse. "I didn't do much with yours. I kind of ran out of time. Sorry."

They didn't speak while they picked through their stockings. Rylie's had a little candy and a lot of lip gloss, which made her smile even though she didn't feel up for it.

She set everything by her feet under the chair.

"You didn't have to do this," Gwyn said as she studied the earrings Rylie gave her. "I'm supposed to be the one giving you a nice Christmas."

She shrugged. It wasn't like Rylie was short on money. She was actually kind of rich, if she considered the value of everything her dad left when he died, but she wouldn't have access to most of it until she was eighteen.

Rylie would have given it all away to cure her aunt.

You could try biting her...

She pushed the thought back. It was way too dark for Christmas morning.

"Did you find all the presents in my closet?" Gwyn asked. She nodded. "Good. Open the big one first."

The big one turned out to be a fancy tablet computer. Rylie gasped. Her aunt hated technology and refused to have gadgets in the house. The thought of Gwyn going into an electronics store was as shocking as the present itself.

"Oh, wow! Thank you!"

"It'll be helpful for school. Don't know if it's any good. That's what the guy at the store told me to get."

"It's perfect. I love it." Rylie leaned over to hug Gwyn. She was even frailer than she had been before going into the hospital, like days without work were making her muscles melt away. The smell of sickness hovered around her.

All it takes is a bite.

Rylie opened her other presents. Gwyn was nothing if not practical, so the theme seemed to be supporting her education. She even threw in a book about preparing for college. Could she really expect to go to college when she could barely control herself in high school? The thought of a werewolf in the dorms was laughable.

But if she stayed home, and Gwyn became a werewolf, she wouldn't need college. It would be even better. She could have a pack.

"What if there was a cure for your disease, but it was really horrible?" Rylie asked. "Like, if there was something we could do to make you better—a lot better, and a lot stronger, too—but it meant hurting sometimes?"

Gwyn glanced at her over the work boots. She was inspecting the soles. "Like chemotherapy for AIDS?"

"No, not like that. Like…" She searched for a way to describe it without using the word "werewolf."

"There's no point talking fantasies, babe. You mean well and all, but I'm not one for dreaming."

Rylie took a deep breath. "I'm not fantasizing or dreaming. Remember when I told you I'm a… you know… a werewolf?"

Gwyn set down the boots and let out a long sigh. "Rylie…"

"Listen to me. Please. I know you think it's my crazy way of attracting attention because I'm depressed or whatever, but it's not." She paused, waiting for her aunt to protest, but Gwyn only watched her with sad eyes. It made Rylie's heart sink. But once she started talking about it, she couldn't stop. "Werewolves can heal almost anything. I haven't gotten sick since I was bitten. Maybe if you became a werewolf too, you could heal the disease."

"Babe—"

"It's better than dying, isn't it?"

"We've talked about this before, Rylie," Gwyn said.

"You have to believe me! Watch this."

She seized the glass on the bedside table and smashed it into the wall. It shattered and sliced into her fingers.

Gwyn shouted and reached for the nurse button, but Rylie grabbed her wrist with her free hand. "No! Wait!"

She held up her bleeding fingers. The skin had been lacerated, but she barely felt it. Her whole arm trembled with heat. She let out a slow breath.

When she wiped off the blood with a tissue, there were no injuries. Her skin was intact.

Gwyn's mouth hung open.

"Look," she whispered, turning her hand forward and backward. Her aunt dropped the nurse button and took her hand instead. Her face had gone bloodless.

"What...?"

Rylie gave a weak smile. "Don't tell anyone. Just... think about it. This could save you."

Someone knocked on the door. Scott Whyte stepped in, holding a big bouquet of fresh flowers and an apologetic smile. "Sorry to disturb," he said.

"What are you—?"

Scott offered a hand to Gwyneth. "I'm Scott Whyte, a visiting psychologist who's worked with Rylie. I wanted to offer my wishes for your good health."

Gwyn's mouth moved noiselessly. She stared at the glass on the floor. Eventually, her polite country upbringing overrode her shock, and she managed to say, "It's a pleasure to meet you."

He handed her the flowers and a little blue box. "I hope you don't mind that I brought a present."

She opened it. A delicate gold chain with a single diamond rested inside on a bed of cotton. "Thank you."

Rylie took a sniff. The flowers smelled normal, but there was a sharp metallic smell around the bracelet that wasn't gold. It looked weird, too. *He's cast a spell on it*, she realized.

"What's that for?" Rylie asked sharply.

He gave her a reassuring smile. "For her good health. Didn't I mention that?"

So it was a healing spell or something. She was torn between gratitude and worry.

"Very kind of you," Gwyn said.

"Merry Christmas, Ms. Gresham." He turned. "Can we talk outside, Rylie?"

She had been about to suggest the same thing. She kissed her aunt on top of the head before following him out the door.

They strolled along the walkway outside the hospital, where nobody would disturb them. It was too cold. Rylie felt fine, and Scott had a thick jacket, but everyone else rushed inside to escape the snow.

"Healing spell?" she asked.

His eyebrows lifted. "I'm surprised you picked that up."

"I'm not stupid. I don't want your weird black magic near my aunt."

"I promise it's benign," he said. "A powerful witch could heal a lot of things, but I'm not powerful, and your aunt is beyond the healing abilities of anyone on this Earth. But she's a strong woman. All she needs is a boost to get back on her feet."

Rylie rolled her thoughts over on her tongue, considering what to say. There were so many answers she wanted to demand from him. But she started with the obvious one.

"Have you heard from Seth and Abel?"

"I have," he said gravely. "They're resting."

Then why hadn't Seth called her? She folded her arms tight across her chest. "Is Abel…?"

Scott nodded. "Yes. He's the killer."

Rylie felt sick. "But… Levi told me that we're all killers. Why would he say that if he's not the one eating people?"

"My kids have had a tough time. Their family couldn't handle them once they got bitten—which was a total accident, by the way. Just a madman who came across them one night."

"How did you find them?"

"They were institutionalized. Even amongst mundane people, I have a reputation for specializing in teens with particular 'delusions,' so I was called in to treat them. But they were gone by the time I arrived. They killed two orderlies, another patient, and a security guard to escape."

Her jaw dropped.

"So they're even worse than me," she said.

"No—none of you are *bad*. We have to put your experience in context: you're sharing a body with a wild animal that was born in the dark times before human civilization. You were never meant to live in houses, attend school, or be locked in cages. If you roamed in a world empty of cities, you would be a normal part of nature. You would be safe."

"Safe from what, exactly?"

"Yourselves." Scott gazed out at the snowy landscape, brow furrowing with thought. "The investigation into the murders didn't implicate Bekah and Levi. Witnesses saw two wolves attacking, so they assumed the kids took the opportunity to escape. When I found them, I made the same offer to them I'm making to you now—to help them heal. So they came to live with me."

"I don't need to be adopted," Rylie said.

"No. You don't," he said.

"My aunt needs me."

"Have you considered that she might heal better without having to worry about you?"

Stung, she kicked a clump of snow over the bridge onto the sidewalk below. "We'll be fine."

Scott nodded. "Abel felt the same when I gave him this offer, too. They thought it would be better to handle it alone, which is why they're leaving, but you don't have to—"

She wheeled around to face him, feeling as though she had been slapped. "Wait! They're *leaving*? What did you say to them?"

"Nothing. This was Seth's decision."

Suddenly, nothing else seemed important. Not Christmas, not her aunt, not the idea of going to live with a bunch of witches.

Scott had to be wrong. Seth wouldn't leave her.

Would he?

Seventeen

Goodbyes

The Chevelle wasn't outside when Rylie got to Seth and Abel's apartment. Icy fingers of fear clenched in her chest.

Had she missed them?

She pushed into the apartment. The first thing she noticed was that all the research had been stripped from the walls. Then she noticed that the futons had been stacked on top of each other and shoved in a corner. Everything else was separated into two piles. One was next to two big backpacks, and the other was going into black trash bags.

Seth stood in the middle of it all, looking through one of his school binders.

"Thank God," she said, moving to hug him. His expression stopped her.

"What are you doing here?"

"Scott Whyte told me you guys were gone. I knew that wasn't right, because..." She trailed off. They weren't ransacking their apartment for fun. When she spoke again, her voice was tiny. "You're not leaving, are you?"

Seth's furrowed brow was answer enough on its own. "Rylie..."

"But you can't go! What about graduation? What about college?"

His face crumpled with pain.

"Some things are more important than that."

"You guys are overreacting," Rylie said. "This is—this is stupid! I mean, yeah, so Abel's made some mistakes, but who cares? He can learn to control himself."

"He's killed people."

She drew in a shuddering breath. Rylie knew Abel was capable of that kind of violence. She wouldn't deny it. But Seth wouldn't let his brother deal with it alone.

"So you're going away to… what? What will you guys get by running away that you can't have here?"

"Your safety," Seth said. "Abel could hurt you. And the pattern of killings will attract other hunters. My mom could come back."

Ugly visions swam through her head. Eleanor had hunted Rylie, attacked her, and tried to murder her. She tied Rylie to the back of her motorcycle and dragged her through the dirt and then fed her poisoned meat to make her crazy.

But now she imagined Eleanor doing those things to Abel, too. Beating him. Tying him up. Pumping him full of silver.

"We'll be safer if we're all together," Rylie said.

He stroked her cheek, eyes pleading. "Think about it. As long as Abel is out of control here, there will be policemen and hunters. They could get him, too. And what if they don't? Abel could kill one of your friends. He could kill Gwyn."

She shook her head, again and again, like denying it hard enough would make it stop. "He loves Gwyn. He would never do that."

"You don't understand. You're different, Rylie. Most werewolves aren't like you."

"But I bit him. I made him like this," she whispered.

"Don't blame yourself. Hey, look at me, Rylie. You can't blame yourself for this. Biting him was self-defense. It's a risk we take when we hunt werewolves."

And suddenly, those horrible images Rylie had of Abel being tortured by Eleanor were replaced with the thought of Seth getting bitten instead. He was perfect in every way she wasn't. He was strong and noble, like a modern knight crusading against the werewolf threat. Getting bitten would violate him. He would be ruined. It was too awful for her to imagine.

Her chin trembled. "I don't want you to go."

Seth responded by wrapping his arms around her, and she clung to his shirt, burying her face in his chest. He was so warm and safe, and he smelled so comforting.

She might never get to smell him again, or be held by him again. Fear ached in her chest.

Rylie grabbed his neck and dragged him down to her level, pressing her lips to his. She kissed him with everything inside of herself, putting every moment they had shared together into it—their struggles at summer camp when she was bitten, the fight against his family, all the times he had looked after her and protected her when she changed.

And Seth kissed her back just as hard. His hands dug into her elbows, pinning her arms to her sides, capturing her in his grip. It hurt. It felt good. Feelings swam through her, confused and disjointed. Her heart was too broken to beat.

"Don't stop," Rylie said when Seth started to step back.

So he didn't.

Rylie had been putting off having sex for weeks. It wasn't that she didn't want it. She did—really bad, actually, way worse than she ever wanted anything ever before. But there was always a reason not to do it. They were never alone at the ranch. Abel was usually at Seth's apartment. And when they really did get time to themselves, it was usually because Rylie was about to turn into a giant, murderous dog. Not exactly sexy.

But now they were alone without anyone to stop them, and she might never see him again.

Passion blazed inside of her like a wildfire, and once it began burning, it wouldn't stop. She wrapped her arms around his neck, locking his lips to hers, and his hands burned hot paths up her back underneath her shirt along her ribcage. His fingers raked along the back of her and skimmed over the bra.

His other hand cupped her breast through her bra. Rylie's breath caught in her throat, and she pulled back a little to look at him. His eyes were filled with heat. It was a little scary.

"Seth—"

He kissed her again, and any thoughts of suggesting that they should slow down vanished from her mind. Every nerve in her body was on fire. He shoved her back until her calves hit the edge of the futons. Rylie lost her balance and fell, dragging Seth down on top of her.

They hit the floor, and she didn't care about how heavy he was or how much their apartment smelled like silver.

She was lost in him, and she never wanted to be found.

He sat back on his knees long enough to strip off his shirt. He was broad and muscled, with faint scars on his ribs. Sweat made him glisten.

Delicious.

The wolf responded to all kinds of hunger—the kind sated by food, the kind sated by violence, and the kind sated with sex. And Seth looked delicious in every way at that moment. He dropped down again, and his lips traveled from hers to her neck, down her shoulder and onto her stomach.

When he came back up to be face to face with her, Seth looked hungry, too.

And then Rylie sank her teeth into his shoulder.

Seth shouted and shoved her away.

She landed on her butt. Instinct took over, and she rose to a crouch, baring her teeth. A growl rumbled in her chest as Seth scrambled to his feet.

He had attacked her.

But he held his hands toward her palms-forward in the universal gesture of peace, keeping his eyes away from hers.

"Whoa, hey, I'm sorry. I wasn't trying to provoke you. Deep breaths. Calm down."

Calm down?

Her blood thundered in her ears. She leaped for him, and he caught her wrist a half second before she could rake her claws down his face.

Seth flung her to the floor. Her head cracked against the wall.

She slumped on the carpet. Everything went fuzzy. Her ears were vibrating.

The sudden burst of pain was enough to jolt the wolf into silence again, but it still took her a minute to remember how to speak again. And once she did, she realized what she had done. "I'm sorry."

When he spoke, it sounded like he was talking from a long distance. "Are you okay?"

"I think so..."

Seth went into the bathroom and flicked on the light. Rylie rubbed her hands over her eyes—where had the claws come from?—to keep from crying.

He was quiet for so long that she had to get up to see what he was doing.

"Oh man," Seth said, craning around to see his shoulder in the mirror. There was a clear circle of tooth indentations in his flesh. "Jesus..."

Rylie's hands flew to her mouth.

"I'm sorry. I'm so sorry, I wasn't thinking, I didn't mean to—did I hurt you?"

She held her breath while he probed the injury with his fingertips. "It's okay," he finally said, blowing out a long breath. "You didn't break the skin."

Rylie collapsed into a kitchenette chair. "Oh my *God.*"

Seth sank to his knees in front of her. "It's okay," he said with more confidence. "I don't know if you could even transform me into a werewolf while you're human."

She wasn't sure, either, but she had a pretty strong suspicion. The wolf wanted to bite him so it could make him pack—just like Abel. If they were all wolves, she could make them stay.

Rylie shivered. Seth was right. They did need to leave.

"I love you," she whispered.

He kissed her. It was gentler this time, and then Seth held her face in his hands and stared deep into her soul. "I love you too, Rylie Gresham. God, I love you. But we have to do this. We have to leave."

He wrapped his arms around her back, and she hugged him tight. Rylie finally let herself cry.

Love wasn't enough. It never would be.

Eighteen

The Other Body

It was well after noon when Tate's black BMW rolled up the street and stopped in front of the gate to his mansion. Levi was waiting outside.

The window rolled down. Tate leaned an arm out to look at him, head rolled back on his shoulders. He wore big sunglasses, but Levi didn't need to see his bloodshot eyes to know he had been partying in the city ever since the dance.

"You," Tate said.

"Me."

"You disappeared at the ball."

"I know," he said. "Sorry."

Tate tipped his sunglasses down his nose. The bloodshot veins made his irises shockingly blue. "Is that all?"

No, it wasn't. But he couldn't explain that he left early because the smell of Rylie's transformation made him and Bekah go nuts. They couldn't help it. Werewolf changes were like a chain reaction.

So he only said, "Yep."

Tate grinned. "Apology accepted."

He shoved the passenger door open. Levi got in while Tate keyed the access code, and their hands joined over the center console.

"You had fun," Levi observed. He smelled more than marijuana—there was alcohol, and a few other chemical smells he didn't recognize. No wonder Tate had taken until Sunday to get home.

"It would have been better with you."

They stopped at the fountain by the front door. Tate didn't park in his garage when Levi was with him, since he loved rubbing his boyfriend's presence in the face of his parents. In fact, he liked it so much that he all but pounced Levi when they got out of the car.

He only put up with it for a few seconds. He knew the performance was for the benefit of the security camera by the front door, not because he was feeling affectionate.

Levi shoved him off. "Save it."

"Prude." Tate snuggled against his shoulder.

He emanated weed and beer so strongly that Levi didn't smell the blood until he saw the shattered windows. Levi grabbed Tate's arm to stop him from going inside. "Wait."

"Huh?"

Tate followed Levi's gaze to the window. A half-second of worry flashed across his face before he started grinning again. "Vandalism. Sweet. My parents are going to be *pissed*."

But it wasn't vandalism. Burglars didn't smell like blood, sweat, and the familiar musk of fur.

"Stay out here."

"No," Tate said.

There was no point in arguing. Levi tried to peek through the broken window before they entered, but Tate shoved his way around him.

The floor of the grand entryway was covered in puddles of water—snow that had been tracked inside and then melted. Precious vases had been knocked off their tables and shattered on the floor. A portrait was tipped at an angle. Ragged claw marks scored the surface of a shattered table.

Levi's eyes fell on the stairs. Even small spatters of blood were obvious to his sensitive nose.

The smears were shaped like paw prints.

"The heck is this?" Tate asked. He wasn't smiling anymore.

Levi made his way up the stairs, ears perked for the sound of movement. He didn't expect to hear the attacker, since he already knew they were long gone.

He hoped to hear a survivor.

But the house was silent.

"Stay downstairs," Levi said.

Tate ran upstairs anyway, hiking his sagging jeans around his hips so he wouldn't trip. "Mom? Dad?"

Levi chased him. The blood turned from smears to streaks as they got higher, and then a small stream that led to the bedroom doors. Tate shoved inside.

His mom was sprawled on the floor, empty eyes staring at the ceiling. She looked like she had tripped and landed on her back, or maybe fallen asleep in an awkward position.

Except that her throat was ripped to shreds.

After Rylie kissed Seth goodbye and watched him walk out the door, she wandered aimlessly around town.

The sidewalks hadn't been shoveled, so she walked on the shoulder of the road. Cars honked at her as they slid past. They were telling her to get out of the way.

Rylie didn't care. She didn't care about anything anymore.

Everything had been going right—as right as it could be, considering what happened since the summer. Things were great at the ranch. She had friends and good grades. And most importantly, she had finally gotten to be with Seth.

Now what did she have?

It had only been a few minutes—or maybe hours, she wasn't paying attention—but she was already lonely. The desolate swaths of snow looked even colder and more hostile than usual.

Everything was Abel's fault. If he had only controlled himself...

But he didn't ask to be bitten, did he?

Her eyes burned with tears, but they chilled as they rolled down her cheeks and quivered on her chin.

Rylie sucked in a ragged breath, leaning against the icy trunk of a tree. The sky and ground were the same shade of white, so it felt like the world had flipped over when she wasn't paying attention. Her head swam.

There were so many people she wanted to blame for Seth leaving—his brother, those Riese kids, even Seth himself—but it all came down to one person.

She had done it to herself.

A car passed and slowed, pulling around her into a parking lot. She blinked at it blearily.

Somehow, Rylie had ended up by the therapist's office. The secretary, Christina, parked in front of the door and got out of her car. "Rylie?" she called, pulling down her scarf so it wouldn't muffle her shout. "Is that you?"

The sight of the older woman rang a distant bell in her memories. She was supposed to be doing something there. Something with her stupid therapist's stupid plants.

She trudged across the street.

"Are you here for Janice's plants? What a coincidence!" Christina said. "I forgot my knitting here on Friday. Come on, I'll let you in."

Rylie wandered inside, staring around at the waiting room without seeing it. The secretary bustled to her desk and shuffled around her drawers. It distantly registered that she was wearing pajamas with penguins on them.

"The water can is in the cupboard," she said.

Mechanically, she grabbed the water can, filled it in the bathroom, and went into Janice's office.

The chessboard was on the table where she had left it, but the shiny black pieces were scattered across the table as though they had been disturbed. A rook was tipped onto its side. Rylie righted it and put it in position.

Scott Whyte's stink was on everything. His stale cologne, his werewolf children, the bizarre herbs he used for magic. It was a slap in the face after their earlier conversation.

But he was keeping his promise to leave. What little he brought to the office was boxed up as he prepared to move on.

She drizzled water over Janice's precious ferns. Some of the leaves were browning and curling in the dry air blasted by the heater. Rylie watched the water pour from the can with a quivering jaw.

Scott Whyte.

If Seth leaving was anybody's fault, it was his.

Setting the water can down hard enough to send water sloshing over the side, she removed the top of the banker's box marked with Scott's name. She shuddered at the smell that washed out.

Everything on the top was normal, boring psychologist stuff—folders and paperwork, mostly. But it was only laid out to hide everything else. A gold bell. Photos of Bekah and Levi from school picture day. A little leather notebook filled with loopy handwriting and drawings of a five-pointed star.

Rylie dug her hand into the bottom of the box, and pain lanced through her thumb.

Gasping, she pulled out what had cut her—a slender knife with a pentagram carved on the side.

A *silver* knife.

Fire swept up her arm. The wound puffed up and reddened on the edges. She flung the knife to the desk and sucked the injury into her mouth.

Her blood tasted like silver. It burned on her tongue and down the back of her throat.

Fury swelled inside of her. That was the last insult.

He kept silver in his office, and it had cut her.

Rylie shoved the box off the desk, and it exploded on the office floor. A snow globe shattered. The bell, the picture, the paperwork—it all spilled across the ugly brown rug.

Whirling, she seized the wooden chair and smashed it into the bookshelf with a shriek. Janice's maidenhair fell. Dirt showered on her boots.

She screamed in pain, in rage, in loneliness. She screamed for all the things she lost—her boyfriend and her life.

And blood spattered on the desk.

Shocked, she looked down at her hand. The wound hadn't grown, but blood poured in a thin stream from her fingertips. The claws emerged a second later, and Rylie gave a cry of surprise that sounded more like a growl.

"It's not possible," she whispered. It was hard to speak with an aching jaw.

The pain in her chest spread. It wasn't loneliness now.

Rylie doubled over. Her elbow nicked the table, and the chessboard fell, showering pieces everywhere.

She couldn't be changing. It was daytime. It was two days after the last moon.

She *couldn't* change.

The secretary stuck her head through the door. "Is everything okay... in..."

Her eyes fell on Rylie and her face went white.

"Get out!"

She didn't have to say it twice. Christina wailed and ran from the office, slamming the front door behind her.

Rylie twisted. Her back bowed, and her heels kicked helplessly against the ground as her spine cracked. She fought not to hyperventilate as the fever took her.

Seth's voice spoke to her: *Be calm, be calm, be calm...*

But thinking of him made her heart break, and she lost any semblance of control.

Her shoulder blades wrenched back, forcing her breastbone forward. Her shoulders popped.

Ribs spread. Her jacket grew too tight. Her hands scrabbled uselessly at her zipper as she fought to free herself with fingers that were no longer attached to normal hands.

And then the wolf erupted.

Nineteen

Surveillance

The snow wasn't as thick twenty miles south of town, so Seth could get the Chevelle up to speed. Empty road stretched in front of him for miles and miles. There was nothing behind him but a lot of regret.

The road used to be his life—his, Abel's, and Eleanor's. They stayed with friends and family sometimes, but they usually tracked werewolves on the open road.

When he moved into Abel's apartment, he hoped he wouldn't move again until it was into university dorms.

But there they were... again.

Abel was stretched in the backseat with his head pillowed on his jacket. He had slept nonstop since the transformation. His backpack was on his lap, and there were a few things in the trunk, but everything else had been left behind.

Including Rylie.

His gloom was distracting enough that it took him awhile to notice the car in his rearview mirror. It started as a distant black speck—nothing to worry about. In the long roads between states, it was normal to have people follow one another for hours at a time.

But the car crept up on him, and a sense of unease came over Seth as it did.

He pulled off on a service road. When the black sedan took the same turn, his heart skipped a beat. "Abel," Seth said. His brother rolled over and mashed his face deeper into the seat. He raised his voice. "Abel. Wake up. We're being followed."

Abel's eyes flashed open in the rearview mirror, awake and alert in an instant.

"What?"

"Get ready," Seth said.

His rifle was in the seat next to him. It was locked and loaded with silver bullets. Seth hadn't been expecting an outside attack—it was just in case Abel woke in a bad mood and didn't recognize him.

Seth stopped on the side of the road. The other car did, too.

"Let's do this," Abel said, gripping a handgun the size of a small cannon.

They got out at the same time, one on each side of the car, and shielded themselves behind the doors.

But it wasn't an attacker waiting for them. It was a black BMW, and Seth recognized the honey-brown hair of the boy who got out with his hands over his head.

"Don't shoot," Levi said.

Abel stiffened, nostrils flaring. His finger trembled on the trigger. Was his gun loaded with silver bullets, too? Seth couldn't remember.

"Why are you following us?" Seth asked, steadying his arm on the side of the car.

Levi looked frazzled. His shirt was buttoned up the wrong way. "We made a huge mistake. You need to see something."

Seth believed him. He lowered his rifle, removed the cartridge, and tossed it in the front seat. But his brother hadn't moved.

"Get out of here," Abel growled.

He crept to the other side of the car and rested a hand on his shoulder. "Give me the gun," Seth said. For a long, breathless moment, he thought Abel wouldn't obey. But then he handed him the pistol. Seth had to check. Silver bullets. That would have been bad. "Okay, Levi. What are you talking about?"

"Come here."

Levi popped the trunk of the BMW. There was a laptop in the back, which he tilted away from the sun so they could see the screen. He loaded a grainy, black-and-white video that looked like a blank sheet of white.

He pointed to one corner.

"This is the driveway to a house in the development back by town. Tranquil Hills."

Seth recognized it. That was where Tate's family lived. He had picked Rylie up from her friend's house a couple times. If that line was the driveway, then the round blurs were the topiaries, and the brighter patches in the back were the house lights.

Abel glowered at Levi. "Where did you get this?"

"I copied it off Tate's security system before the cops arrived," he said.

"Why were the cops there?" Seth asked.

Instead of answering, Levi skipped ahead in the video. He resumed normal speed when a small human figure crossed from one corner to the other. The timestamp was for the previous night.

They vanished. He opened another video from a different angle. The figure approached the front door of the house. It was still blurry, but Seth thought he recognized that stride. He would have known Rylie anywhere.

She punched her fist through the window, elbowed shards of glass out of the way, and went into the house.

"Oh, hell no," Abel said.

Levi loaded a third video from another camera. Seth didn't want to see it.

"Why were the cops there?" Seth asked again.

"Tate's mom was killed." Levi's voice was flat and emotionless. "Her throat was torn out."

His ears filled with a roaring sound as the blood rushed to his head. Abel grabbed his arm. The painful press of his fingers into the muscle was the only thing that kept him upright.

The third video was from inside the entryway. Rylie's indistinct figure changed. It was abrupt—a twist of the spine, a seize in her legs. Then Rylie was gone, replaced by the wolf. Seth stared at the timestamp as if he could will it to change.

She couldn't change between moons. Could she?

Someone else ran into the grainy video. He didn't recognize the dark hair and dress, but he assumed it was Tate's mom. The wolf chased her upstairs where the camera couldn't see.

There was one more video on the folder. When Levi moved to click on it, Seth closed the laptop.

"That's not possible," he said.

"Silver poisoning. It drives a werewolf crazy and makes them transform out of control." Levi thumbed the plug in his ear. "Bekah and I use silver to change at will, but we don't let it into our system. She's bad. She must have had it a long time."

Seth flashed back to the night his mother shot Rylie and embedded a silver bullet deep in her thigh.

He thought he had pulled all the fragments out.

But he was wrong. That was why her nails fell out whenever she got mad. She must have been changing between moons.

"Seven bodies," he muttered.

Now eight.

"Hell," Abel swore.

Levi nodded. "We have to find her."

But Seth had already run back to grab his rifle.

Bekah called Levi when they reached the outer edges of town. He listened to her speak, and his face went pale.

"We'll be there in a few minutes."

"What is it?" Seth asked. He was riding in the passenger seat of the BMW, which he was nauseated to discover belonged to Tate. He had to crack a window to be able to breathe. Abel followed closely in the Chevelle.

Before Levi could respond, the flashing red and blue lights of a police cruiser zoomed past them, squealing with sirens. It drove a cold spike of fear into Seth's chest.

His heart sank even lower when they followed the police onto the street of Seth and Abel's apartment.

They passed the old strip motel and stopped in front of the office of Rylie's therapist.

Levi parked across the street in an alley. Abel looped around the block and pulled up behind them. The police car they followed to the scene wasn't alone. It was joined by three other cruisers and an ambulance. People in uniforms milled around the parking lot, looking aimless and chilly.

Despite the late evening cold and two feet of snow, everyone in town seemed to have turned out to see what had the cops excited. A dozen people were gathered on the sidewalk. It was practically a mob, given the small local population.

Seth got out of the car for a better look, but hung at the back of the crowd. People were whispering. He caught words like "assault" and "crazy."

He felt the itch of an approaching werewolf an instant before Bekah came around the corner.

"What happened?" he hissed.

She dragged him to the corner for a better view. "Look."

The back of the ambulance was open. An old woman he recognized as the secretary sat on the tailgate with a blanket draped over her shoulders. Even from across the street, he could see she was shaking.

Abel loomed over his shoulder. His face was fixed in a grim mask that made him look decades older than nineteen.

"Did Rylie get her?"

"No. We got lucky. Kind of."

"Kind of?"

"I listened in on her report to the cops. She saw Rylie go inside, then found her halfway furry a couple minutes later. Police think the secretary's lost it, but there are people who will hear her story and know it's true."

People like Seth's mom. Heck, people like *Seth*.

"We've got to find her," Abel said. "*Now*."

Bekah and Levi both nodded. Seth was surrounded by gold-eyed gazes. "We can do that," she said.

The siblings raised their noses to the breeze and sniffed. Seth wished he could smell like they did. His own sixth sense for werewolves didn't do any good when he had a couple right next to him.

Out of the corner of his eye, he saw Abel lift his head to do the same. Chills crawled down Seth's spine. He pretended not to see it.

"I have her smell," Levi said. He sniffed Seth's collar. "There's wolf all over you."

He jerked away. His hand twitched for his shoulder, where his rifle usually hung, but it was still in the car. Bekah stepped between them.

Sirens went off again. Two cruisers peeled into the street.

A pair of sheriffs left on foot with German Shepherds. Seth heard a low growl from behind him and wasn't sure who was doing it.

"Let's split up," he said. "We'll cover more ground."

They returned to the alley. "We'll be faster on foot," Levi said, dropping his jacket and pulling his shirt over his head. He threw his clothes in the BMW, completely unembarrassed to strip in front of others. Bekah ducked behind the corner to do the same.

Seth watched in sick fascination as Levi transformed. It was so much faster than Rylie's changes. His body shuddered. His face extended at the same time his tail emerged, and fur swept down his body in seconds.

Not a minute later, a werewolf stood in front of him.

Levi was smaller and shaggier than Rylie. Somehow, he had the same serious expression as a wolf that he did as a human. It took all of Seth's control not to grab for his gun again.

Bekah trotted back to them, shaking snow out of her fur.

"Whoever finds Rylie..." Seth hesitated. He felt weird talking to dogs. "Don't hurt her."

Bekah huffed in acknowledgment and nudged her brother.

They ran to the end of the alley and separated. Abel got his gun out of the car and double-checked the clip. "I'll get her," he said, stuffing it in the back of his jeans and pulling his shirt out to hide it. "Trust me."

He ran off in pursuit of Bekah.

Seth watched them disappear, feeling strangely helpless. Hunters, police, and Abel—all searching for his girlfriend, who was alone, sick with silver, and starving for meat.

He had to find her first.

Twenty

Changed

Rylie woke up in a snowdrift.

She groaned and cradled her head between her hands. Her tongue felt like it had doubled in size while she slept, and her skull was ringing. She couldn't seem to focus her eyes.

The world was washed out and gray. It was cold, it was dark, and she had no idea where she was or how she had gotten there.

Standing on trembling legs, Rylie scanned her surroundings for familiar landmarks.

Was it the morning after a moon again? What had happened to the last two weeks? And why was she in so much pain?

She staggered to the shelter of a tree where the snow wasn't as thick, trying to gather her jumbled thoughts. Sadness gnawed between her ribs. The grief was so immense that even her momentary amnesia couldn't wipe it out.

Rylie was missing something—or someone—important.

Flies buzzed in her skull. She tried to shake them away.

Where was Abel? Where was her pack?

A breeze lifted, and a smell caught her attention. Meat. Rabbit, bird, or something else? She wasn't sure. There was too much information on the icy air, from distant humans to her own sweat and the heavy chill of snow.

She even smelled rivers and stone and pine trees, but there was no forest nearby.

Tracking the smell through the skeleton trees, she shoved past bare branches and ignored the drip of icicle water on her shoulders.

The body was crumpled between two big rocks. Rylie got on all fours to study it. She couldn't make sense of all the legs and twisted spine. Was it a human? A deer?

To her, it looked like nothing but prey, and she was so hungry. Always hungry now.

She couldn't eat this meat. It had been dead for hours.

Rylie recalled the feeling of an esophagus collapsing between her teeth.

A distant howl broke the air. Her head jerked up.

"Abel?" she asked, wrapping her lips carefully around the sound. But that wasn't possible. She could feel the moon slumbering now, and knew it wasn't at its apex or nadir.

Then why had she changed?

Too many questions.

"Holy mother of God," someone said.

She glanced over her shoulder. The wolf had been too distracted to hear the approach of boots on snow. A man stood behind her, someone gray-haired and old. He wore the flesh of animals and carried lead.

More prey. Good.

"What are you doing out here, honey?" he asked with the accent of someone who had lived his entire life in the country. "Jesus, you're going to freeze." He moved to strip off his coat.

Rylie bared her teeth, and he froze.

They stared at each other for a breathless moment. Would he shoot her? She was faster than him, but she wasn't sure she could outrun a bullet.

Her mind was suspended between human and wolf. One wanted to flee. The other wanted to attack.

The wolf won.

She leaped. The hunter didn't expect an attack from a naked girl. He yelled and tried to jump out of the way, but she was like lightning. Watching him raise his gun—too slow, much too slow—she darted around him and attacked.

Her fingers bit into his jacket. Her momentum sent them both crashing into the snow. His gun flew from his hands.

He flailed his fists, and pain exploded in her temple.

Rylie reeled.

He scrambled to his feet. His eyes were wide, his pulse raced, and his skin poured the delicious scent of fear and adrenaline into the air. "Sweet Jesus!"

By the time she flipped onto all fours again, he had already fled through the trees and left his gun behind.

He was fat and slow. She could catch him.

The pain in her temple radiated through her body, making her stumble midstep. Her spine cracked.

Not again.

Rylie's hips popped and her knees made a sound like shattering glass.

She couldn't balance with her legs twisted in reverse. Sagging, she barely caught herself on a boulder and almost fell straight into the body. The pain of the transformation cleared her head for a moment. Human Rylie was relieved to realize the body was furred—a deer, not human.

But her relief was short-lived. Once she remembered killing the deer, she recalled killing other prey. Things that weren't furry. Things that cried in human voices.

"Help me," she whimpered. "Somebody. *Please.*"

Nobody was listening.

Where was Seth? Why wasn't he waiting for her? He was *always* waiting.

He's gone.

Grief overwhelmed her as she remembered their last, desperate kiss, the press of his body against hers, and the taste of her own tears.

He wouldn't be waiting for her ever again.

Rylie struggled to focus on keeping her bones and muscles from changing. She thought of human things. Walking on two feet. Hands and fingers. Clothes, school, cars, cities.

Pop. Crack.

The skin of her cheeks stretched as bones pushed out. Her ears ached. Rylie grabbed her face in both hands, and a clump of white-blond hair fell where she touched it.

Groaning, she tried to focus on breathing. Counting numbers. *Anything.*

Gwyn. The ranch. Home.

That was where she needed to go. It was the only place she could be safe and secure, now that her pack was gone.

Rylie needed her aunt.

She dragged herself away from town, which was nothing more than a faint glow of light beyond the hills, and moved toward the smell of cows and chickens. It took everything she had to keep moving—when had she grown paws?—without succumbing to the pain.

Her focus was so strong that she didn't notice when the wolf's mind slid over the human's. And she didn't notice when her blood dripped on the snow.

•☽•

Gwyn was settling in for the night when her phone rang. She gathered her robe around herself, stuffed her feet in her slippers, and padded to the place the phone was mounted on the wall. She had been waiting for it to ring all night since she got back from the hospital to find her niece missing.

"Rylie?" she answered.

But it wasn't a girl on the other end of the line. "Really sorry to bother you, ma'am," responded a deep voice she recognized as Abel's.

Her worry sharpened into something close to fear. "Have you seen Rylie? I checked myself out of the hospital, and she's not at home or picking up her cell phone."

"You checked out?" he asked. "Why would you do that?"

"I got sick of the hospital and thought it was high time I came home. Where is she?"

"I don't know."

Gwyn leaned against the wall and shut her eyes. She had been so sure Rylie was hiding at their apartment. "What's going on? Is she—?"

He cut her off. "Lock the doors. Lock the windows. Don't let Rylie in if you see her."

"*What?*"

"You heard me."

Not many things made Gwyn worry. The barn at her first ranch had burned down and killed half her cattle, and she still hadn't lost her cool. She hadn't even panicked when the doctors gave her diagnosis.

But between Rylie's demonstration earlier and Abel's warning, she was suddenly afraid. It was an alien feeling. She didn't like it.

"Is this a... a *werewolf* thing?" she asked.

Abel went silent. When he spoke again, his voice had a new edge to it. "What do you know?"

Gwyn gave a shuddering laugh. "I don't know much of anything these days."

"I'm headed your way right now. I think Rylie might be, too. Don't let her in."

He hung up. She clutched the phone to her chest, staring around the dark house.

Gwyn lived in a dull world, and she liked it that way. She didn't believe in ghosts or God, and all she expected to wait for her after death was a fast rot in the cold ground. In her darkest times, she didn't turn to Jesus, and nary a prayer passed her lips to ask for help or forgiveness. She didn't feel a need. Gwyn never had the faith the rest of her family did.

What she knew, she knew well—the earth and the cattle and the satisfaction of honest labor. The kind of things she could see and touch.

The rest of it wasn't real. It couldn't be.

As if to punctuate her thoughts, a shriek fractured the air beyond her walls. It didn't sound like a coyote.

Her hand shook as she hung the phone in its cradle. Taking a deep breath, Gwyn walked to the window and pushed back the curtain. The porch lights made it hard to see into the night, so she flipped them off and waited for her eyes to adjust.

Another shriek. But this time, she saw what made the noise.

Something climbed her hill—something thin and pale and four-legged.

Cold shock slapped Gwyn like a winter wind.

The sight of her niece crawling through the snow was enough to make Abel's warning vanish from her mind.

Gwyn flung open the door and plunged outside in slippers. Her weakness was replaced by sheer adrenaline.

"Rylie!"

The girl twitched and shuddered like a sickly dog. There was something wrong with her—something worse than being on her hands and knees in three feet of snow.

She slipped and slid to Rylie. "What are you doing, babe? Get up out of there!"

But then she saw what was wrong.

Her niece—the sweet baby girl who used to ride her pigs like ponies—had grown a long, bare tail, more like a rat than a wolf. Her face was bleeding. Her hair was patchy. She left a trail of crimson in the snow behind her.

"Help me," Rylie whispered.

And then she collapsed in the snow with a scream.

Her body contorted. Her hands clawed at the sky. Fur slid from her skin like grass growing too fast, and her screams turned to howls.

Don't let her in, Abel had said. He'd been onto something there.

"Jesus Christ," Gwyn breathed.

She didn't wait for Rylie to finish changing. At the bottom of the hill, she was closer to the fields than home, and she wasn't sure her legs could carry her up the slope. So instead, she ran for the paddock.

Her legs were sluggish with cold and her slippers had soaked through. She kicked them off at the fence and threw herself over the side.

Every panting breath made pain spike through her lungs. The doctor said she could resume normal activity when she felt up to it, but he probably hadn't meant running form werewolves.

Rylie's screams cut off.

Gwyn threw a look over her shoulder as she unlocked the stable door. Whatever moved in the snow wasn't a girl anymore. It was huge and hulking and faster than anything she'd ever seen.

She ran inside and slammed the door.

Something crashed into the other side and made the latch shudder.

The horses shifted in their stalls, restless and worried. Gwyn threw the bolt on the door and went to the nearest horse—Butch, good old Butch, who didn't fear anything—and climbed on his back as the monster struck the stable doors again.

He danced on his hooves. She gripped his sides between her knees and hugged his neck.

"Go! Get moving!"

The door cracked on the third blow. On the fourth, the stable was blown wide open.

As a wolf, Rylie was almost as big as Butch. She wasn't shaking anymore. She looked powerful and inhuman—there was no little girl in those luminous gold eyes.

The horses shrieked. Butch darted out of his stall, and his motion caught the gaze of the wolf.

It lunged.

Butch jumped out of the way, and Gwyn clung to his back as they burst out of the barn into the chilly night air. The wolf roared behind them.

She didn't need to kick him to get Butch moving. He had somehow forgotten he was old and turned into lightning. He sliced through the snow, Gwyn's silver braids streaming behind them.

The wolf's teeth snapped at Butch's tail. Its paws were thunder pounding against the ground.

They tried to jump the fence. Butch's hind hoof caught, and he lost his footing. He fell out from under her, and Gwyn cried out as she was flung off his back.

Hitting the ground was like smacking a brick wall face-first. All the breath left her aching lungs.

And the horse screamed.

Gwyn couldn't get to her feet fast enough. Her body was too cold, too weak. But she got up in time to see jaws close on Butch's throat.

Blood sprayed. His hooves kicked helplessly.

A distraction was a distraction. Gwyn couldn't do anything for him—hell, she couldn't do anything for herself, either.

So she ran and didn't look back.

Seth dove through the snow, rifle hugged to his chest. The night was pierced by the occasional howl, but he couldn't tell who it was or what was happening. Was it Bekah and Levi communicating over long distances? Or was Rylie shrieking with fear and pain?

It felt like he made no progress traveling through the vast plains of snow. He ran for an hour without seeing changes. Everything looked identical in the dark, except for the occasional tree or passing car.

But then something moved among the dark shapes of an orchard. For a breathless moment, he hoped it would be Rylie. Then the figure drew closer, and he saw it was a man—terrified and bleeding.

"Hey!" Seth called, intercepting him.

He stopped the hunter by grabbing his shirt, and the older man stared at him with wild eyes as though he didn't really see anything.

"Let me go!" He wrenched himself free of Seth's grip and shook a finger at the north. "There's something out there. It looks human, but—holy mother of God, it tried to eat me!"

"What was it? What did it look like?"

"A naked girl," the hunter said. "There was a deer—a dead deer—"

Seth clenched his fists. "You'll miss the road running that direction. Head east. Go!"

He didn't have to say it twice.

The man fled and Seth headed for the trees.

A dead deer. He hoped that would be the only dead thing he found that night.

A tingle in the back of his mind made him change trajectory before reaching the orchard. He recognized some of the hills now, as well as the iced-over stream that sliced through the land. Gwyn's property was close, maybe just two miles away.

And the wolf was close.

His heart pounded as he scrambled up a ridge overlooking a valley filled with black, leafless trees.

Something moved on the opposite hills. A pale figure ran through the snow, and he realized with a jolt that it was Gwyn.

A bathrobe flapped behind her. Her feet were bare, and she moved sluggishly.

Seth jumped down the ridge, struggling to get through the snow that had collected at the bottom. It was too thick. He stumbled gracelessly down the slope.

A moment later, Gwyn slipped. Her cry pierced the air as she fell.

Seth froze, holding his breath as she tumbled head over feet. She bounced off a rock and came to a stop at the bottom.

Gwyn's body didn't move.

"No," he muttered as he slid another foot down the ridge. "No, no, no—"

Another form appeared on the opposite hill—a dark patch against the snow. It was moving fast, but not as quickly as a normal werewolf should have.

Rylie circled around her aunt. She was always beautiful and terrible as a wolf, but she looked like a nightmarish echo of her usual self. Her fur stuck up in spikes, blood caked her face, and she shivered with every step. Her eyes rolled. Drool dribbled from her lolling tongue.

All signs of silver poisoning. Seth should have known.

"Please—don't do this," Gwyn whispered. It was so quiet that he heard her from the top of the ridge.

The sound of her voice jolted him into motion again. He slipped down as quickly as he could, fighting his way against sliding drifts.

Rylie growled. Golden eyes focused on Gwyn. Werewolves couldn't resist sickly, weakened prey.

But she should have been different. She should have known not to attack her aunt.

He lost his footing and sank waist-deep into the snow.

The wolf roared and jumped at Gwyn.

"Rylie!"

A honey-gold blur exploded from the trees and barreled into Rylie's side an instant before she could bite Gwyn.

Both wolves went flying. She leaped to her feet immediately, twisting around to snap at the wolf that attacked—which was Levi, judging by the size—but he darted out of her reach. He swooped in to snap at her legs.

Werewolves were terrifyingly fast when they fought—faster than any human could hope to match. His eyes couldn't even track them through the valley.

Another wolf appeared. Bekah ran to Gwyn and stood over her body, sticking her nose into the older woman's face and neck as if to see if she was still alive.

When Levi and Rylie's fight rolled near, Bekah stood between them, guarding Gwyn's body.

Levi tore into Rylie, shrieking and snapping.

Bones cracked. Blood spattered.

Werewolves healed fast enough that minor injuries didn't sway them. But Rylie was mindless and brutal. The fact that Levi changed at will and kept his mind put him at a disadvantage.

He couldn't keep up with her. She bounded around him, ducked under his belly, and shoved him off his feet.

Rylie's teeth closed on his spine mid-back. He yelped.

Seth finally pulled out of the snow and reached the bottom of the valley.

"Rylie!" he shouted.

She froze, focusing reflective yellow eyes on him. The entire right side of her face twitched. Her ear flopped. Her shoulders rolled and seized.

Did she recognize him? Or had the silver destroyed what little of her mind remained?

He put the rifle on his back and walked toward her slowly, holding his hands out palm-first. No sudden movements. "It's okay," he said. "It's me."

Rylie shivered. He stretched his fingers for her nose.

Behind her, Levi moved.

He lunged and shoved her into a tree with his massive head, breaking the moment of calm. She yelped.

"Wait!"

But he had lost her attention, and he couldn't get it back. Levi bit at the thick ruff of fur around her neck, and Rylie swung a huge paw tipped with diamond-sharp claws. It sank into his side. His scream was almost human.

Levi collapsed. Seth glimpsed something glistening on his belly.

She had gutted him.

Bekah howled and leaped for her brother, leaving Gwyn unguarded. She lay flat on the snow, too weak to move.

Rylie whirled. Seth tried to get in the way.

The wolf was too fast.

A gunshot whip-cracked through the air.

Blood splattered on Rylie's flank, and she stumbled before reaching her aunt.

"No!" Seth roared, whirling to see who had shot. A silhouette stood on the ridge with a gun braced in both hands.

Abel.

Rylie struggled to stand, but he fired again and hit her in the shoulder. The silver bullets were far more effective than Levi's bites. She slid onto her side again with a cry that broke Seth's heart.

He scrambled toward her, but Bekah darted out of the trees and blocked his path with her body. Abel jumped down, much more gracefully than Seth had, and caught his arm.

"Get off of me!"

"You can't go near her," Abel said, voice gruff. "She could bite you."

Fear and fury gripped Seth. He elbowed his brother in the gut and swung a hard uppercut. The crack of fist meeting jaw wasn't as satisfying as it should have been—Abel only grunted and didn't let go. His hand was like an iron shackle.

He glimpsed Rylie beyond Bekah. She writhed and whined with the agony of silver burn.

"You shot her!" he spat, shoving Abel again.

"I wouldn't have had to if you shot her first." He stepped back and stuck his gun in his belt. "The Riese kids will take care of her. We've got bigger worries for now."

A few feet away, Gwyn moaned. Seth had completely forgotten about her.

Abel lifted her from the snow very gently. She didn't react to his touch. She was bleeding, too, but it looked like it was from a few cuts and scrapes rather than a bite. It wasn't as worrying as the blue tinge to her skin.

Another cry made him turn. Bekah had Rylie pinned down.

"Forget her," Abel said. "You can't do anything, and we have to get Gwyn to the hospital five minutes ago."

Seth hesitated as he watched Rylie. Her skin rippled and her teeth snapped at the air.

He couldn't get close without risking a bite.

"Hurry up! Help me!"

So he followed his brother, leaving Rylie to the mercies of the wolves.

Twenty-One

A Funeral

Seth stayed at the hospital with Gwyneth for three long, horrible days.

It seemed like the least he could do when he couldn't be with Rylie. He didn't know where she was or if she had become human again, and nobody was talking to him—not the Rieses, who seemed to have gone missing, or even Abel, who only showed up every few hours to check on Gwyn's status.

Of course, he didn't have anywhere else to go anyway. They had already given up their apartment.

Gwyn asked to see Seth on the afternoon of the third day.

She looked like she had been beaten up, which wasn't far from the truth. She gestured for him to sit in the chair beside her. "They tell me that Rylie hasn't been around."

Seth glanced over his shoulder to make sure nobody was listening. He shut the door into the hallway before sitting down again. "People are taking care of her. It's okay."

"So it's true," Gwyn said dully. "It's all true."

"I'm sorry," he said, even though he knew it was no comfort after everything she had been through.

"I don't want to be bitten."

He blinked. "What?"

"Rylie offered to…" Gwyn's thin hands clenched on her bed sheet. "She thought a bite might cure me. If that's what it's like, I don't want any of it."

The fact that Rylie had been thinking of making another werewolf should have worried Seth, but nothing shocked him anymore. Not after everything that had happened over the last couple of weeks.

"It's not usually like that," he said.

But was that really true? Wasn't that the kind of behavior he expected from most werewolves?

Gwyn broke him from his thoughts. "She's not coming back. Is she?"

"I don't know," Seth said. He scrubbed a hand over his face. "I just don't know."

He spent one more night stretched out between chairs in the waiting room, dozing lightly with nightmares chasing around his skull. When he saw Abel go into Gwyn's room, he wasn't sure if it was another strange dream or reality.

Around two in the morning, someone cleared her throat. Seth looked up to see Bekah with Abel loomed behind her. So he hadn't been dreaming.

He stood. "Is Rylie—?"

"She's okay," Bekah said in a low voice. "We got out most of the bullets, and she finally woke up this morning. Human."

"Where is she? Can I see her?"

Bekah shifted, glancing at her cell phone and stuffing it back in her pocket. "Look… Seth. I don't think that's going to happen. Rylie's refusing to see anyone." She grimaced. "Especially you."

Seth sat back down hard. "But—"

"She's agreed to go to California with us," she went on. "We'll take good care of her. I promise. Maybe in a few months…"

"A few *months*?"

Abel stared hard at the window, jaw clenched so tight that thick cords stood out on his neck. "I'm going, too."

"Can I come?" Seth asked, but he could tell the answer by Bekah's expression before the words even left his mouth. "Then what am I supposed to do? If my brother is going, and my girlfriend is going…"

She shrugged helplessly. "You're a kopis. The other werewolves and witches wouldn't feel safe with you there."

"And someone's got to look after Gwyn," Abel said. He still wouldn't look at Seth. "I already talked to her. She wants you to stick around, finish school, and help her sell the ranch. She'll need someone with her now that Rylie is…" He trailed off, cleared his throat, and fell back into silence.

"She wanted me to give this to you." Bekah gave him a folded piece of paper and a weak smile. "Guess this is it. Goodbye, Seth."

She ghosted out of the waiting room, her long white jacket trailing behind her. Seth's fist clenched on the note.

"Abel—"

"It's either this or letting Mom kill me," he said. "I messed up. It's too late to fix me now. But… maybe those witches can help with the control thing."

Seth grabbed his shoulder. "We can do it together. We don't need anyone else."

"Don't you get it, man? Rylie killed people. I killed people. This is our last chance to make it better." Abel finally met his eyes. His dark irises were veined with gold. "Don't worry. I'll look after Rylie."

There was nothing else to be said, after that. They weren't much for hugs or long goodbyes. His brother punched him in the shoulder, and Seth shoved him back.

"See you around," Abel said.

"Yeah. See you."

Seth waited until he was alone to unfold the note Rylie left him. It looked like it had been torn out of a journal. The ink was smudged with a teardrop. Only one line had been written in the middle of the page:

I'm so sorry. I love you. -Rylie

•◐•

The funeral for Tate's mother was held on a bright, windy day. Rylie watched them from the hill beyond the cemetery gate, arms hugged around her body against the cold. As the county commissioner, a lot of people had shown up to grieve. They were black spots against the glaring white snow.

Even from a distance, Rylie's sharp eyesight could pick out Tate. His face was crumpled, his cheeks were ruddy, and he had traded out his usual jeans for the kind of suit his mother begged him to wear. He called it "the livery of The Man."

He was crying so hard that he was sweating despite the cold, and his hair stuck to his forehead. Tate's dad had an arm around his shoulders to comfort him, but he wasn't in much of a better state.

Why should he be? Their family was ruined.

Rylie had never seen Tate cry before. She knew how that grief felt. It hadn't been long since she stood beside her dad's grave as he was buried.

But this time, she was responsible for the funeral.

When she woke up, Scott told her that she had killed people. She couldn't remember anything, but she had to believe them when she woke up after being trapped as a wolf for three days straight. She didn't know what to think or feel or say anymore. It felt like her heart had turned to ice.

Her hands twisted on a silver pendant. It stung her skin even though it was plated with rhodium to prevent serious burns. Scott Whyte said she had to wear it everywhere. He hadn't been able to tell her if it would give her control.

The honk of a horn echoed over the hills. She turned her gaze to the road beyond the trees and saw a white van idling on the shoulder.

Her time was up.

Rylie took a long last look at Tate, trying to memorize his face. She would never see him again.

"I'm sorry," she whispered, wishing it would carry over the wind and find his ears. He stepped forward to drop flowers on his mother's casket. Motors whirred and lowered her into the ground.

That wasn't how she wanted to remember him, but maybe it was what she deserved.

She limped to the van. Rylie had woken up with two fresh bullet wounds—one in her hip and one in her shoulder. Scott and Bekah had pulled out all the silver they found, but it still burned when she moved. They said they had a doctor that could fix it when they reached California. For now, she winced with every step.

Levi slouched next to the open door of the van. His eyes were red, too, and he glared at her when she drew near. Rylie stared at her toes, trying to decide what to say.

"I don't know if..." she began.

Levi interrupted her. "I don't want to hear it."

Her mouth snapped shut and her cheeks burned.

Rylie climbed inside. The smell of other wolves made her tense, but her hand gripped the pentacle tight and anchored her enough to stay human. Scott and Bekah were chatting in the front seat. They sounded happy. Normal.

Levi climbed in and shut the door. He wouldn't look at her. Rylie stared out the tinted window at the darkened world, watching the cemetery gates recede.

"We have one stop before leaving town," Scott announced.

Nobody spoke as they drove to Gwyn's ranch. She slid low in her seat, clutching the pentacle so hard that the edge dug into her hands.

"I don't want to be here."

"We're not going inside. It will only take a second."

Scott parked at the end of the driveway, and Rylie couldn't resist. She peeked over the side of the door to drink in one last look at the ranch house, the barn, and the pastures.

Home. Her heart ached for it.

She wanted to go up that hill, drop her muddy boots by the back door, and immerse herself in the warmth of her aunt's kitchen. She wanted to snuggle under a blanket with Gwyn to keep warm. She even wanted to help her muck out stalls.

But that was over. She ruined it.

Figures emerged from the front door, and she felt a small jolt to see Gwyn, Seth, and Abel. Her aunt looked frail. She held Seth's arm for balance.

"Do you want to say goodbye?" Bekah asked, twisting around in her seat. Her face was sad and sympathetic. It made Rylie feel sick.

She couldn't say goodbye. If she spoke to Seth, she would have to see his disappointment. She couldn't handle that.

Rylie hadn't even left him a note.

"Are you sure you don't want to go? We can wait a few minutes."

"No," she said.

They didn't try to push. Rylie sunk into her seat again and hugged her knees to her chest.

Her heart of ice couldn't stand to think about Seth. He would thaw her, and she would have to feel the pain. All of it. The guilt of having killed, the knowledge she had ruined her life, and the realization she might never see Seth again.

She was so immersed in her miserable thoughts that she didn't notice Abel's approach until he opened the door. His backpack was slung over one shoulder.

Their eyes met. Everything she felt was mirrored in his expression—remorse, anger, fear, sadness.

"Make room back there," Scott said.

Levi moved over, shoving his bags into the cargo space so Abel could get in.

Bekah threw a nervous glance at Abel. "Last chance, Rylie."

"Let's go," she said. "Now."

Seth started the engine again. The sound must have carried up the hill, because Gwyn and Seth stopped by the door into the ranch. A voice echoed over the air just before Abel slammed the door.

"Rylie?" Her aunt was calling to her.

Rylie's heart shattered as the van pulled away, and she couldn't hold it back anymore. A sob ripped out of her. It hurt to cry, like getting stabbed in the chest. She couldn't stop once it started.

"It's okay," Bekah said.

She shook her head and wiped her cheek with her hand, but there was no holding back the flood.

No. It wasn't okay. It wasn't okay at all.

The van rounded a corner, and the ranch—with Seth, Gwyn, and everything good about Rylie's life—disappeared with it.

About the Author

SM Reine is a writer and graphic designer obsessed with werewolves, the occult, and collecting swords. Sara spins tales of dark fantasy to escape the drudgery of the desert, where she lives with her husband, the Helpful Baby, and a small army of black familiars.

Sign up to be notified of new releases
and get a free ebook!
eepurl.com/eWERY